THE
DROWNING

'A work of rattling and serpentine suspense from a national treasure of the screen and now, most assuredly, the page. Gripping and sinuous and so, so good. Brown can see every inch, every grain of this truly unique surf-and-sand-noir world. He knows well this creepy coastal stuff. The tales behind the tans. The deadly games behind the dunes. And all the twisted paradise screams and sins that get sent out to sea.'

— Trent Dalton

Bryan Brown is known as an actor, having appeared in over eighty film and television shows. He has worked in some twenty countries including his home country of Australia and the United States.

Sweet Jimmy, consisting of seven short stories on crime, was released in 2021. *The Drowning* is his second book.

Praise for *Sweet Jimmy*

'Uniquely Australian and uncommonly good, I could hear the author's voice in every spare, haunting line. More please.'
— Michael Robotham

'My friend Bryan Brown, quite apart from his other manifold talents, turns out to be an excellent writer. An authentic voice; highly imaginative yet completely believable, with a flair for fully realised characters and a gripping narrative . . . a great storyteller. This is utterly baffling. I'm furious.'
— Sam Neill

'Bryan Brown makes an impressive entry into Australian literary ranks with his first collection of short stories . . . A terrific collection of gritty tales, recommended.'
—*Canberra Weekly*

'Brutally funny and distinctively Australian . . . Bryan Brown is going to be a force to be reckoned with on the literary scene.'
—*Woman's Day*

'Dazzling . . . strikingly original. If Brown ever decides to leave acting there is clearly another career waiting for him.'
—*The Sydney Morning Herald*

'A colourful, bold and cheeky collection of suburban Aussie noir stories.'
—Book'd Out

BRYAN BROWN

THE DROWNING

ALLEN&UNWIN
SYDNEY • MELBOURNE • AUCKLAND • LONDON

Allen & Unwin
Cammeraygal Country
83 Alexander Street
Crows Nest NSW 2065
Australia
Phone: (61 2) 8425 0100
Email: info@allenandunwin.com
Web: www.allenandunwin.com

Allen & Unwin acknowledges the Traditional Owners of the Country on which we live and work. We pay our respects to all Aboriginal and Torres Strait Islander Elders, past and present.

 A catalogue record for this book is available from the National Library of Australia

ISBN 978 1 76106 980 2

Set in 12/18 pt Sabon LT Pro by Midland Typesetters
Printed and bound in Australia by the Opus Group

10 9 8 7 6

 The paper in this book is FSC® certified. FSC® promotes environmentally responsible, socially beneficial and economically viable management of the world's forests.

THE
DROWNING

THE
DROWNING

1

David ditched his bike by the side of the track behind a gummy. Same place as before. Then pulled a bit of bullshit grass and stuff over it.

Better to hide it. Never knew who might be along and David wasn't keen on getting in the bad books with you know who. The drug heavies.

David found the entrance a month or so back when he was pissing about with nothing to do. He'd skipped school cause there was bugger all going on. Always bugger all going on. David didn't blame the teachers. There was always a bloody great racket going on in the classroom. Most of the kids wanted to learn but there was a mob who didn't give a shit and blew it for everyone else. So the teachers just told you what pages to read and left it at that. So why bother going?

Moira would whip him if she knew.

She wasn't gonna know. He'd be back before dark.

Thing he did love learning was his language. Indigenous language. And he wanted to improve. You bet he did. And he was getting good at it. Gumbaynggirr was his mob. Funny how if there's something you want to learn then the easier learning is. David tried to explain this to his older brother Wayne but Wayne wasn't ready. He didn't have time to learn. Bit of a silly bugger was Wayne. Kept getting into strife. But he was starting to quieten down now. Had to, Moira said.

David thought if he got good enough with his language then one day he could be a teacher. Teach the other kids their language. David loved that idea.

And now David was back here deep in the forest.

Because last time he found the shed.

And he wanted another look.

You had to be bloody careful being out this far. So many padlocked gates. DO NOT ENTER. And guns for sure.

But David was smarter than the average fuckwit. He knew how to be sneaky. It was in his blood. Silent as.

Last time David thought he might find a patch. Gunja patch. Plenty of gunja patches out here in the Parks. National Parks. Get a couple of pockets full. Make a buck.

But.

Better.

He found the shed.

No one about. Just a shack and a shed covered in gal iron.

All closed up.

So sneaky David snuck up for a look. Pretty hard to get a look inside but then he found a hole in the gal.

Wow and didn't he love what he saw. Classic. And now he was back for another look.

And take a picture.

Blow his mates' minds.

David lay on his back and wiggled his way under the barbed wire. Too easy for a blackfella. Then he made his way from gummy to gummy, bent low and quiet. Didn't know who owned the joint but they wouldn't want him there, that's for sure.

There were gummies and bushes almost all the way to the shed. There'd been bloody great bushfires all through the forest but somehow some places escaped the fire. No rhyme or reason. Just however God wanted it. That's if you believed in a god. If not, it was luck. Good or bad. David couldn't believe how fast the forest was coming back. Green shoots everywhere. If you looked closely you could see the black trunks behind the green. Nature was amazing, David reckoned.

He was about to dash to the hole in the gal for a geek when he noticed the van. That wasn't there before. Better be careful. So he was. Stopped. Lay down in the grass and watched.

Lay there. Waited. Nothing going on. And then the door to the shack opened and a big bloke came out, walked around to the side of the shack, bent down and lifted a trapdoor. Heavy steel. Went down steps. Must be a room below.

David thought this was a good time to piss off but he couldn't help himself.

Who was this fella?

Sort of recognised him. Sort of. Could be one of them surfer fellas at the coffee shop. What was that place called? The Basin yeah. A hangout for the old blokes. All looked the same too. Old blokes. Anyway, thought he'd seen him about a couple of times.

And then up came the fella holding a rope. He was leading something. A girl. The end of the rope was tied around her throat. She just followed him. Wasn't fighting or anything. Maybe it was some game. Some adults' game. David had seen porn. Everyone had. Some strange sick stuff goes on there. The fella led the girl to a spot by the shack and tied the rope to an iron stake belted into the ground. The girl sat on the ground while the fella sat a frypan on a steel plate that he swivelled into place. He lit a fire underneath the plate. Then he emptied the contents of a bag into the frypan. And stirred.

The girl said nothing. She was dressed but her clothes looked pretty wrecked. Hanging off her.

Her hair was matted. David couldn't see her face. Then the bloke went inside the shack leaving the girl sitting there. She didn't move. Didn't even look around. Just sat.

David ran to the side of the shed. Keeping down. He had to take a closer look. This was weird, man. Really weird.

David thought maybe the bloke had gone to get plates or something but how long does that take. He was sure taking his time. David watched the girl. No movement. Didn't even move her arms. Still, like a dummy.

David took out his phone and looked through the hole in the gal. Yep, still there. Still a classic. So he snatched a photo then turned the phone off. Didn't want that going off and giving him away.

Where was the bloke? He'd been inside for at least ten minutes. David worried the food would be burnt through. You can't leave stuff burning over a flame without watching it. Moira had told him that.

Where was the bloke?

And then a bag came down over David's head. A rope around his body. Pulled tight.

He couldn't move. Shit scared. Literally.

He felt his bowels open and the shit ran down his leg. David screamed.

He was dragged along the ground. Then picked up.

And now his head was in the water. With a hand pushing it down. Down.

He couldn't fight back. The bloke was too strong. David wanted to grow up strong.

People respected you if you were strong. But he wasn't going to grow up strong. Not now. And he could say goodbye to any more learning of his language.

David knew he was going to die here in this water.

———

When the boy stopped struggling, the bloke pulled him out of the dam. Laid him on the ground. Made sure he was dead. Then he carried the boy past the girl around to the shack. Leant him against the wall.

The girl waited.

Terrified.

And then she heard it.

An almighty wailing.

Loud. From deep down. From the darkest place.

The shack door opened and closed.

When the bloke returned he carried two cups and a plastic container holding water.

He passed one cup to the girl. She took it. She had to look at him. Couldn't help herself. And she had to speak.

'Did you kill the boy?'

'He was an intruder.'

They sat in silence.

He spooned food from the frypan into a bowl and put it by the girl. He poured water into her cup.

She took some water.

'You want more water?'

She nodded her head.

'Didn't hear you.'

'Yes.'

'And?'

'Please.'

He poured water into her cup.

Now she didn't dare look at him. Didn't know if he might lash out.

So she looked at the ground. Kept quiet. Gulped down the food from the bowl. Knew she had to keep it down. Wasn't easy. Never knew how long to the next meal. Sometimes twice a day but not always. Whenever he felt like it.

She wondered what he was thinking. What he was going to do.

It was the first time someone had been to the place. Well as far as she knew.

There may have been others. Sometimes she thought she heard a car but down in the room you could hardly hear a thing.

And if the boy had discovered the place then maybe others knew about it and maybe others would come. And others would find her. And finally she would get out of this hell. She had to hold on to that. The hope that someone would come. She had to hold tight on to that no matter what. It had to end.

The frypan was empty. He poured water onto it, kicked the steel plate to the side and held the pan over the fire. Scraped it with a fork. Cleaned it. Sort of. Then he stood.

'Pour some water on your face. Don't want a dirty face under me, do I?'

Then he went back into the shack with the frypan and bowls.

She wanted to scream.

Scream the forest down.

Scream the whole fucking world down.

But she couldn't.

It would cost too much.

And then he returned.

Took the rope off the iron stake.

'Up.'

She rose.

He led her to the trapdoor.

'Down you go.'

He followed her down.

Then he pulled the trapdoor shut.

2

They found him washed up on the beach. A kid. One of the locals doing her morning walk with her dog came across him. Actually the dog found him. Was up ahead of her tugging at something. A body. Sun had only just come up. She rang the cops. Waited. Others doing their walk joined her.

A gaggle of them and their dogs. Staring. The chatter about 'Who was he?' 'Did anyone know him?' 'Poor kid.'

They pulled the kid away from the water's edge. He was definitely dead. Looked dead.

And then the cops were driving towards them along the beach. Only one car. Four-wheel drive. Police sign on top. Not even flashing.

It was at the three-kilometre mark she spotted him. It had a sign. Said three kilometres. Three kilometres from the Point.

The Point, where most of the blokes surfed. And the girls. A lot of girls surfing now. And good. Not like the early days when there was hardly a girl to be seen. Well, not in the water. On the beach for sure.

Wanda was a beachie in those early days. In her bikini, sunbathing while the boys surfed. Great days. Salt and sun and fun and lust. They all had plenty of that.

And now Wanda was waiting for the police, to show them what she'd found.

———

The beach had been closed off. Two more vehicles were called to the scene of the drowning.

That's the word that filtered back. A kid had drowned down near the three-kilometre mark. Wasn't even a big swell day. Beautiful spring day. Moderate swell. Offshore. How could you ask for more?

David could ask for more. Like his life back. But that wasn't going to happen. Word spread out into the water. Didn't take long.

'An Aboriginal kid has drowned along the beach.'

Slowly the surfers drifted in. Everyone wanted to see the young fella.

———

The three vehicles crept past the onlookers. Up onto the concrete driveway from the beach to the car park. They stopped. Everyone surged. Pushing to get a look. And some did get a look. A side window showed David in the back of the cops' four-wheel lying along the floor.

Towels had been placed over him.

The cop asked people to move back away from the vehicle. Said statements would be taken from anyone who might have seen the young boy this morning. Or anything that could be helpful with their inquiries into the drowning. Then the cars moved off away from the beach.

After the cops had buggered off, Wanda led a bunch of the locals to The Basin. Coffee and gossip. Wanda was the centre of attention. That's for sure. You couldn't get near her.

There was more than one coffee shop but somehow The Basin had become the place to go chat after a surf. Maybe it was because of the service. Service with a smile. That always works and Benny had the smile and the chat that goes with it, and he surfed.

Benny had been coming to this part of the north coast of New South Wales for as long as he could remember. When he was a kid, he and his mum and dad and brother and sister camped here every Christmas. Such a great camping ground right next to the beach. Benny believed the camping grounds had saved the coast. There were tons of them all the way up the coastline. Packed with kids and parents barbecuing and laughing and boozing and swimming. Didn't get any better than that. Stopped bloody great high-rises from taking all the best spots. Yep, saved the coastline, camping grounds.

Back then Benny never thought that one day he'd have the best coffee shop going round. But he did.

And now Wanda was holding court. Not that Wanda didn't always hold court. Plenty of front with Wanda. Physically as well. She had always filled out a swimsuit well. And loved it.

But this was terrible. He couldn't have been more than fifteen, the young boy. He looked like an angel, she reported, and she'd definitely seen him about. Not a lot. Skateboarding or riding his bike with his hands up in the air and laughing. Most remembered him. Terrible.

———

Wanda had grown up a good Catholic schoolgirl. St Brigid's, out Hurstville way. Fifteen k's west of the Sydney CBD. Middle class. Sort of, with a bit of working class chucked in there. Wanda's mum was Spanish. That's why Wanda was so good-looking. The old man was an Aussie. They lived in a brick house at Kingsgrove, not far from the school.

Wanda was a looker. No doubt about that. And the blokes from the Catholic boys' school next door were always sniffing about. But Wanda chose Barry. Wanda was fifteen. Barry was sixteen. Good at school, good at sport and good-looking. And he made her laugh. They'd go to the beach on Sundays. To Cronulla. Cuddle on towels. Have a kiss. And that was all, because Wanda was a good Catholic girl.

But things changed. Wanda started hanging out at the milk bar after school. Where the local public-school boys hung. She stopped getting the train home with Barry. They didn't fight or anything. Just sort of parted. Barry noticed Wanda started painting herself. Lipstick and stuff and pulling her skirt up past her knees. She was getting a lot of attention at the milk bar and you could see she liked it. Would wave to Barry as he passed. Not a looking-down-your-nose wave but. Just a friendly wave.

Then she started sipping black velvet through a straw. She loved black velvet. They all did. Coca-Cola and vanilla ice cream and lime cordial. Wanda would look up at Greg while sipping. With her big brown eyes. Greg was the leader of the boys. No question. Charismatic. And Greg would put his arm around Wanda. Squeeze her. She'd smile.

Wanda found life so exciting now. She was the queen. Had to be the queen because Greg was the king. He drove. Greg could get his old man's car to go out Saturday nights. Not that they went far just down to the river. Parked. Had sex. Greg taught her like he'd taught the other girls from around the area. That went on for a couple of years. Wanda failed her finals. Greg hadn't even bothered to sit for his. Wanda was under Greg's spell.

Of course that ended. They both moved on. Then there was a failed marriage, and now for the past ten years Wanda had been living here on the coast. Loved it here. She didn't have a boyfriend but there was the odd fling. Got to get what you can when you're fifty plus. And maybe even a little more. Yep, Wanda had a secret.

———

Ken looked down the beach from the car park at the Point. Top day. Only about ten of them out. Plenty of waves for everyone and Ken knew most of the blokes. Be all locals in the main. That would change when school hols came and the camping ground would be full and little grommets everywhere.

All on the inside stealing your wave. No respect. Some of the blokes didn't care. They reckoned it was good seeing the kids riding. Makes them healthy, and anyway there were plenty of weeks when there were no kids. Just local kids, and they had respect. Been taught it. If you were a local kid you got taught it.

Ken had a thing about respect. He'd been taught it. Had it belted into him by his father. Nearly threw up whenever he thought of that word. Father. 'Gutter snipe', that's what his so-called father called him. Always accusing him of things he hadn't done. Not going to accuse the other kids, his 'brothers'. That's what comes from being adopted. Only adopted him so the kids had someone to play with. Someone to blame. Someone the real kids had to blame. The kids that had come out of his mother's you know what. Not like him who was handed over to her.

Yep, time for a surf. Good time for a surf. Everyone was coming in. All itching to see the drowned kid.

He watched the three cars slowly working their way along the beach. He'd been watching from the beginning. Watched the cop car going out. Leaving tyre marks in the sand. It was sort of beautiful.

Well, let's get it right, everything about the beach is beautiful. But on a day like this and with what was happening it was different beautiful. Almost spiritual. Probably the right word, spiritual, seeing as it's about death.

He watched as the other two cars went up to the body. And now they were all coming back with a little crowd following.

Yep, good time for a surf. Likely to be the only bloke out, seeing as all the rest want in on what's happened. All want a look at a dead body. People are weird.

Ken wandered down to his van and unstrapped his board.

Benny was going to make a quid today, for sure. Might have to bring a few casuals in. Whatever happened to that other girl? Wondered about that a few times. There'd been a Danish girl worked at The Basin for about a month. Then three weeks back she disappeared. Just vanished. But to where? Who knows? No one asked about her. Must have moved on. It's a big country. Easy place to lose yourself in. And guess she lost herself somewhere in it.

The Basin was packed. He knew this would go on all week, maybe longer. Maybe for the month. Maybe through until Christmas. No, that wouldn't be a good idea. Put a dampener on Christmas holidays. As if. They'll come running, wanting to hear all about it.

'Is this the beach where the kid drowned?'

Put them back on the tourist map.

Haven't had anything big since the Chinese ship ran aground. And that was up near the three-kilometre mark, six years ago. What a coincidence. Maybe the three-kilometre mark is a doomed spot. Of course it isn't. The body could have washed up anywhere. Could start the rumour though. Gives the place an intrigue.

And wasn't the grounding of the Chinese ship a number. It was there for about six months.

Authorities didn't know what to do with it. The locals did. They swarmed all over it. Diving and jumping off it. They weren't supposed to but who was going to stop them.

Story is, about two hundred Chinese all dressed in suits fled the thing and went racing down the beach and off into the forest. Knocked on residents' doors, showing a piece of paper with a phone number written down and asking for them to phone.

14

Must have been all arranged. How they got so close to land without being spotted no one knows, but early in the morning, there it is. Grounded.

They say they were all rounded up but most reckon that's bullshit. No one had any idea how many there were exactly.

Caused a sensation. Increased trade.

So might this.

This drowning. This drowning of an Aboriginal boy.

Yep, Benny was going to have to ring a couple of the backpackers who'd applied for work.

Always backpackers around. Loved it here. Plenty of young surfers around happy to play romance with the backpacker girls. And the girls are good workers. Enough of them have passed through here over the years. Plenty have worked at The Basin. Maybe that's what happened to the Danish girl, she found a bloke. Romantic.

3

There was a knock at the door. It woke Adrian. What time was it? Then a key was turned in the lock and the door swung open. Sheila wandered in, bucket and mop in hand.

'You around Adrian?'

'Yep. Getting up.'

He'd always been a night person. Old habits die hard. Real hard. Hard was his mantra.

From way back. From back when he collected. You had to be hard or they'd walk all over you. And you were expected to be hard. That's why you were on the payroll. And work was done at night. Maybe because life is scarier at night. He'd knock on the door. No mucking about.

'I'm here to collect.'

And dark behind him at the door. Sometimes they'd try it on.

'I'll have it next week. Bit short at the moment.'

And before they knew it their back was slammed up against the outside wall with Adrian's dial up against their dial and Adrian saying just one word.

'Now.'

And know what? They'd find it.

But that was many moons ago. Collecting.

'I'll start in the kitchen. Give you time to get rid of the juice.'

'Have trouble with the word piss, don't you, Sheila?'

Sheila didn't answer. You learnt not to answer back too often with Adrian. Could be funny. Could be nasty.

Nasty was in him.

But Sheila needed the job. Rents had been on the move on the coast. And the movement was up, not down. Some mates had been forced out cause of the higher rents.

They'd lived here for years, but now the cities were moving to the regions and the pressure was on. So don't answer Adrian back. Smile and clean the joint.

Shame he was like that. Might have fucked him if he was nicer. Nearly did, a few weeks back after a party. Ended up being a grapple in the park. Nice grapple, though. Good body. All the blokes had pretty good bodies. It was the surfing. Kept them young.

Even if most of them were pensioners now. They reckoned you needed a pensioner's ticket to surf the coast. Anywhere on the coast.

Adrian had surfed Sydney. Maroubra. Easy to get a job working for the boys if you came from Maroubra. Everyone knew Maroubra blokes never took a step back. Not in their blood.

Adrian's dad was a hard nut too. Told Adrian stories of his time up the Cross before he became a cop, working for Perce on the door of the Forbes Club in the late sixties. Bloody well-run club, the Forbes. And why not? Who was going to start a blue in the Forbes? You'd be beaten to a pulp by one of Perce Galea's boys. Those were the days, Adrian reckoned.

Adrian was feeling it. Been a late night. Made him think of hard again. Different hard though.

———

It hadn't been easy carting the kid through the bush and then down to the beach. He'd waited until well dark before he set out. Made sure he'd stripped the kid down to his jocks. Had to look like an accident. Crossed the highway and then drove along the dirt road that paralleled the beach. Drove careful. Lots of holes. When's the council going to get off its bum and fix this track? What are taxes for? And now lights. Headlights. High beam. Passed.

Fuck.

What to do?

Turn around?

No, continue. Don't get paranoid.

There was an area where the blokes parked their cars when surfing down the beach away from the Point. He pulled in. No one there. Why would there be at this time of night?

For a good reason that's why. For a sly kiss or cuddle or maybe the odd root on the back seat. Everyone's done it sometime or other. Obviously what the other car was up to. But clear now. Better wait. And he did. Waited fifteen. Nothing happening. Can't wait all night.

He hoisted the kid out, over the shoulder, and headed for the water.

Sand didn't make it easy. Made it very fucking difficult. Why did the little prick have to see what he saw? Girl on the end of a rope. Well, wasn't going to be able to explain that away, so only one thing to do. And he did it. And he did it quick. Kid didn't know what hit him. Should have minded his own business.

He stood at the water's edge. From here you could see the lights from the village. Twinkling. If only the twinklers knew what was going on down their beach. He laughed. Was pretty fucking funny thinking that. Needed to go down there after this to see a twinkler. Delivery.

He dropped the kid onto the sand. Water splashed onto him. The tide was going out so it would take the kid with it. Out there where it's dark. It'd bring him back later for sure. Maybe here. Maybe up the beach. Or down. But first he had stuff to do.

He laid the kid on his back and slid him into the water, holding his head back so water could get into him. Different water than the dam water he drowned the kid in. He'd tried back at the house to get as much of that out as possible. Couldn't get it all out. But most kids around here have a bit of dam water in them.

He walked the body out through the froth until it was up past his waist and then he pushed the body further out. Watched as it floated away. Wouldn't take long to sink.

When he couldn't see it anymore he splashed back to the beach. Kept looking out. Couldn't see a thing. He was about to move off when he remembered.

Reached into his pocket and took out the kid's phone. Kid had turned it off. Thought it smart to turn it back on. Then he hurled it out to the body. Kid needs his phone.

4

The Basin was still open at six. Meant to shut at four during the week but not today. The drowning was like a magnet. It wasn't party time. Nothing like that. The mood was low-key. Sombre. But a lot of locals had lobbed down wanting to get the inside.

Quite a few remembered the young fella. He was around. Not in the water though. Nobody had caught him swimming. So, what the bloody hell was he doing going in the ocean?

Had he gone in last night or super early this morning?

Brian Slaviero said he'd been doing a house appraisal at around six o'clock last night down by the beach but saw no Aboriginal kid. Reckoned the drowning might affect house prices. Brian had a dark sense of humour. Eastern European background. It was strange that, Benny reckoned, how adversity translated into dark jokes.

'Put a sock in it, Brian. Ain't funny.'

'Just saying, Ben. Anyone see the kid?'

'I was here unpacking until late and I didn't see any kid.'

'Unpacking what? Basin's closed Tuesdays.'

'Unpacking the coffee you bastards pour down your throats. Doesn't walk in and put itself away.'

'Get us another, mate.'

And they all laughed.

'Brian's paying,' called Wanda.

Benny smiled and went to get a round of coffees.

They all wondered when the cops would come calling.

———

Benny finally kicked everyone out at seven. Shut up and drove a mile down the road in his van to his home.

Wanda waited out front for a lift from Brian, who was taking a leak. Brian's wife wouldn't be back for a few days.

Adrian walked past. Said g'day to Wanda and continued to the beach for a late swim.

Ken drove past in his van having finished an evening's surf.

———

David's gran was called Moira. She was still crying. Couldn't stop. She loved her David.

David's mum was a mess. Had been for a few years now. Drugs and alcohol. Not uncommon up the coast, black or white. His dad had been killed in a lorry accident while working on one of the bypasses. Bypasses everywhere now going up the coast. Don't see any towns anymore. It's faster but not as interesting. But hey, the world's got faster in everything.

David's gran took over. Took over raising David and his brother and sister. She was their rock.

They loved her to death and she loved them to death. That's why she was worried when David wasn't home for dinner. He'd often go mucking around with mates after school. Having a good time but never missing his dinner. Moira was strict. Rules. One was to be home for dinnertime.

Moira rang him a dozen times but no answer. Rang his mates but no one had seen him. Actually hadn't seen him all day. Didn't make it to school. That did not make Moira happy and he'd know about it when he did get home. After dinner Moira rang the police. Told them he'd been missing all day. Police didn't show a lot of interest.

'If he doesn't show up by morning give us another ring and we'll come out. Probably smoking gunja somewhere. He'll be back.'

But David didn't come back. His dead body was found on the beach at the three-kilometre mark.

———

Adrian knew this could be a problem. Needed to be sorted now. He knocked on Benny's door.

'Hi, mate.'

'Hi, Adrian.'

'Come in?' Adrian asked.

'Yeah, sure.'

And Adrian walked into Benny's lounge room. Benny closed the door.

'Beer?'

'Sure.'

Benny went to the fridge and came back with two beers. He handed one to Adrian. Waited.

'We got a problem.'

Benny didn't say anything. Took a swig of his beer.

Adrian continued. 'This drowning. Cops are going to be sniffing.'

Adrian took a swig. 'Need to hold back on the weed.'

That didn't sit well with Benny.

'You're joking, aren't you, Adrian? There are always cops around. It'll mean fuck-all.'

And Adrian explained that this time was different. That the boys out back had a fair-size set-up going on. And there were always boys out back. Drug boys. And they did not need cops sniffing. Not now.

Benny was pissed.

'Mate, this drowning is here at the beach, nowhere near the forest. Me passing a couple of bags to locals is not going to fuck anything.'

'Benny, you will lay low. Do not sell a single joint. Or some big fucking tattooed bikies will be coming by to say hello. Got me?'

Benny took another swig, then finished the bottle. He looked at Adrian.

They had a good thing going, he knew that. A bit of weed for the locals. An extra grand a week to help with the rent. Rents were going up, so every bit helped. He knew Adrian was overreacting, but no point arguing.

Adrian had made the connection. It was Adrian who would get belted if anything went arse-up.

'Yeah, okay, mate. I'll keep the cupboard locked until this passes over. Won't be long. Just a drowning. Another beer?'

Adrian didn't answer. He got up and went to the door. Opened it and turned to Benny.

'They don't muck around, Benny.'

Then left and closed the door behind him.

Benny went to the fridge and grabbed another beer.

This was a bugger.

It was a conversation with Adrian about the locals liking a smoke that had led to their little association. Adrian was only trying to help and Benny knew that. Adrian had a history. That's what it was, history. Adrian was over his bad old days. Long over them. But he knew where to suss some good weed from out back and Benny knew how to offload it.

There had been a delivery last night too. Later than usual. Must have been near ten o'clock. Just as Benny was finishing up at The Basin.

Maybe Adrian was right. Don't want this to get bigger than needs be. Yep, keep the cupboard locked.

5

The cops spent most of the next day down at the beach. Came into The Basin. Questioned everyone. They showed David's picture about. Wanda was right, he did look like an angel. No one had much to offer. It looked like death by misadventure. Drowning.

'Didn't see anything strange, out of the ordinary, around the beach on Tuesday night?'

And always the same.

'No, mate. Home watching telly. She's quiet here at night. Nothing to do.'

Of course Wanda and Brian had chatted. What about the van they'd passed on the way back from the beach? Should they mention that? Meant they'd have to answer questions about what they'd been up to in the dark, down the back of the beach.

Brian had already stated he was doing a house appraisal around six. Can't say that took forever and that's why he was out late. And what if the other car says they saw a woman in

Brian's car? Fuck, it's getting complicated. Best to shut up. The van they passed wouldn't have had fuck-all to do with the boy's death. Just as he didn't.

Why didn't he go straight home after the appraisal?

Because he got horny, didn't he. Ended up meeting Wanda.

And he knew Wanda was up for it. Up for a fucking. Down the parking area back of the beach. He certainly wasn't going to do it at home. Not stupid. Nolene could walk in at any time. Never did say when she'd be back. And certainly not at Wanda's place. That would be all over town in minutes. Everyone sees everything.

Except an Aboriginal boy drowning.

———

Benny was definitely not going to mention his visitor. The Basin was closed Tuesdays. That meant restocking for the rest of the week. And there was plenty to restock.

Told the cops he packed the van with goodies for the shop and worked there until late and saw nothing. Nothing strange.

Well, the delivery was late and that was strange, but that's not being mentioned.

And it's true the delivery fella is a strange bastard. All those blokes out bush are.

Every so often the bloke popped into The Basin for a coffee. Benny thought he was spying on him. To who?

Paranoia.

That's what happens when you get involved with criminal activity.

For fuck's sake, this wasn't criminal activity. It was a bit of weed for the locals. Should never have got involved with the fella.

Bloody Adrian.

Benny had no idea where the fucker lived. Somewhere out bush. Who knows where? You could get well and truly lost out there, or shot if you happened upon the wrong place.

Years back there were plantations of weed. Semitrailers came to cart the stuff away. But once helicopters and those special cameras started being used then things changed. Changed big time. Smaller plots, hidden in gullies mixed with lantana out in the forests. Guessed that's where his stuff came from that Adrian had arranged.

It wasn't just dope anymore that the bikies were interested in. No, it was ice. Renting houses out bush and setting up labs, so they say. Some say it's brought in from China and India. Who knows? Plenty of unemployed on the coast. And ice got you through the day. And fucked you completely. Big money in getting people fucked.

Fuck, what am I doing? I've got to get out of this. Telling Adrian, no more. Too dangerous.

Benny needed a nap.

He was getting stressed.

———

Ken had seen something. He wasn't exactly sure what he'd seen but he'd seen something that night.

He liked his evening surf. Didn't get it all to himself though. There'd be one of the boys out if a wave was on. There was always someone out until dark.

A lot of surfers reckon not in the water until after sunrise and out before sunset. But Ken will surf until it's black and if it's a full moon then anything goes.

It wasn't a full moon but there was good light. Three-quarter moon. Must have surfed until eight or quarter past. Only one out then. He came in, dried off and went through his yoga routine.

Yoga in the evening meant a ripper sleep.

Sleep of the dead.

Not the best thought, given what's happened. A drowning.

Then a series of wind sprints on the beach and push-ups. One hundred. He could still do it.

Ken had done push-ups his whole life. Never missed a day. Started when he was young. Needed to be strong.

Only one time gave a kid at school a belting. Never needed to again. No one chanted 'You're adopted. You weren't wanted' where Ken would hear. Not unless they wanted a belting.

After the push-ups, as Ken was walking to his van, he spotted movement up the beach.

Couldn't quite make it out. A figure near the water's edge. Maybe. Or the moon playing tricks with the light.

Ken gave it no thought then but he had today. He sure had, because he remembered that the figure was around the three-kilometre mark.

And now he was staring up there.

Did he see something?

Yes or No.

And should he say something?

Ken walked to his van and tied his board on.
He'd sleep on it.
A yoga sleep.
Sleep of the dead.

6

The cops had been to talk to Moira. They were respectful. She knew one of them. Local cop, Sergeant Gallagher.
He was well regarded by the Aboriginal community. Didn't
come down hard on the kids, not like a few cops before him.
Hard bastards. Some were mean as well as hard.

They sat at the kitchen table. Moira made tea.

Moira was proud of how she kept her home. Having a
home meant a lot. Her parents hadn't been that lucky. Moira
was one of the Stolen Generations. She had been taken from
her mother at four and fostered out. Aborigines Welfare
Board. They decided Moira's parents were negligent. Took
Moira while her mum was in hospital giving birth to Moira's
brother. Later he was taken. Another fostering.

She remembered saying, 'Are we going to see Mummy?'
Over and over.

'Are we going to see Mummy?'

And then at the foster home.

'Where's Mummy?'

And then you give up.

But you don't forget.

When Moira was reunited with her mother, she was overcome. Tears flooded both their faces. But there was pain as well. The pain of remembering. It came racing back.

'Are we going to see Mummy?'

And there was pain now. David was gone.

———

Sergeant Tommy Gallagher enjoyed being a police officer on the coast. He knew he wasn't a city cop. Knew that's where they'd send him after graduating from the Academy, but luck was on his side. Sure, he went to a big town. In fact, Newcastle was a city. City of Newcastle. Nothing like Sydney, though. Anywhere in Sydney was going to be packed with people. Packed like it had been out at Parramatta where he grew up. Tommy liked Parramatta. Fun place to grow up. Rivers and bush around Parramatta. And that's where his love of water and swimming came from. His parents were great. They made sure every Christmas the family went out of town. Somewhere up or down the coast and somewhere with ocean. Tommy really fell in love with the ocean and, if he was lucky, a local girl.

In one of those towns up the coast Tommy fell in with a bunch of Aboriginal kids and boy were they wild. Not bad wild but game bastards wild. They knew the best places to swim with the best trees to jump off. And fishing. Where to fish. What bait to use. How to cook it.

So he let it be known at the Academy that he wouldn't mind being sent to an area with an active Indigenous community.

Newcastle was where they sent him for five years. And he did pretty good there but he ached for somewhere smaller. Up or down the coast, he didn't care. Eventually he got his wish and now he was here. And now he was interviewing an Indigenous lady about the death of her grandson, David, washed up on the local beach.

Moira told Sergeant Gallagher and the other cop that she didn't understand how David had drowned in the ocean. Given he wasn't a big one for the ocean. Sure, he'd swum in the ocean, but he and his mates were river rats. They knew every bend of every river round this part of the coast. They knew the big rivers and the creeks. And the places to dive and the places to fish. The places to lie in the sun talking bullshit and the places to hide.

Moira knew that David loved an adventure and could easily go off on his own and find his own fun, but most times he was with mates. He loved his mates. She couldn't work out why he'd skipped school. To do what?

And his bike was missing. His pride and joy. It wasn't a new bike or anything but it was his. He'd saved for it by doing odd jobs for neighbours. Took him just on a year and then he found what he wanted on Gumtree. Everyone found what they wanted on Gumtree. How amazing was Gumtree? Who invented Gumtree? David wished he did.

It was a mountain bike. Pedal Ranger 3. Black. It was a steal. Only one hundred bucks. The owner had wanted one-twenty but took a hundred. David was stoked. Not stoked now. David was dead now and the bike was nowhere to be seen.

7

There was a bloody lot of people at the funeral. It was held on the island in the middle of the river about two kilometres from the mouth that pours into the ocean. It had history, the island. History as an Aboriginal reserve. Many of Moira's generation had lived on the island until the early fifties when the island was leased off and the reserve moved.

Moira looked out at the crowd. About two hundred people. Surprised her. Didn't realise her little David had touched so many lives. Lot of whiteys too.

Two boys played the didge.

Moira and the uncles and aunties and cousins walked slowly through the crowd to behind the coffin. They stood looking out at the crowd seated on chairs or on the grass. A light breeze took the heat away. The deep trumpeting sound of the didge set the mood. Great sound, the didge. Nothing like it. Moira's heart ached. *David. David. David*, it ached.

Flowers were placed on the coffin and on the grass beside.

Then the smoking began. One of the uncles carried burning leaves in a small bucket, waving the smoke over the family as he moved past them.

Then the sounds from the didge finished.

——

Brian Slaviero wondered what the idea of the smoking was. Strange, he reckoned, waving smoke all around the place. What if a bloke had asthma?

'Everyone to his own,' his old man used to say.

Brian didn't like sitting among the mourners. It wasn't his idea to come. It was Nolene's.

'Of course we're going to the boy's funeral. Pay our respects.'

'But we don't know him, for Christ's sake.'

'He drowned on our beach.'

'It's not our beach, Nolene. What are you talking about?'

'If it was one of the young white boys you'd be going, wouldn't you?'

'Go on, call me racist. That's what you're getting at, isn't it?'

'Shut up and get dressed, Brian. We are going.'

And Brian did. And he wished Nolene had stayed away for another week.

Could have had more fun with Wanda.

Got lonely at the house on his own. Used to like sitting on the lounge watching *The Crown* with Nolene. Wow is that family a mess. Royal family, royally fucked.

But now he and Nolene were sitting on the grass in front of the coffin looking across at the boy's family.

Wanda had come with Benny. Benny had shut The Basin for the day. Thought it was the right thing to do. They sat to the side with Ken, who had joined them.

Wanda was impressed by the ease of the family. Not hysterical. Calm and loving.

The blokes were all dressed in black. Black pants and black shirts. Some with black jackets. They all had red bands tied around their heads.

'Must be a cultural thing,' Wanda said to Benny.

'What must be?'

'The red bands around their heads.'

'Suppose.'

There was a microphone set up beside the coffin. The coffin was covered with the Aboriginal flag. Black and red with the yellow sun.

Wanda was sure one day it would be the Australian flag. Too striking not to be. Thought she might write an article on the subject for the *Courier* one day. She did the odd article. Picked up five hundred bucks each time.

She liked writing. Always had. At school she knew how to string a sentence together. It came naturally. And a writing course at uni sharpened her up. Got in as a mature-age student. Mature. Bloody hell, if they'd only seen her in the back of Brian's van they might've used another word other than 'mature'.

A young man stepped up to the mike. This was Wayne, David's brother. Wayne tried to speak but couldn't.

Then he leant on the coffin and kissed it. And spoke to David.

'I miss you so much.' He took a deep breath. 'You will always hold a special place. You will always be the star in my sky. You were too young to die. You didn't have to die. I love you . . . miss you . . . love ya.'

Wayne stood beside the coffin. Broken-hearted. One of the aunties walked up to him and put her arms around him. Wayne slumped into her. She led him back to the family.

Ken watched Wayne and felt for him. He hoped he was behaving like he'd agreed to. The family didn't need any further trouble. David's death was enough for them all.

Sergeant Tommy Gallagher had arrived early to help in setting up. Make sure no one else was using the area.

He also wanted to be aware of everyone who turned up. Even though the cause of David's death was drowning, something still nagged at him. Couldn't get rid of the nag.

Now David's sister, Marcia, walked to the microphone.

She told the crowd about her little brother. About his little life. His favourite television shows. His respect for old people. How he loved playing poker and his love for old classic cars. She told a funny story how one time he'd got chilli all over his hands from picking and had scratched his nuts afterwards only to then jump up and down screaming and raced and jumped in the dam. This got a bit of laughter from the mob.

A young fella took over from Marcia. Couldn't have been more than ten or eleven but he had a poem for his bro.

Nolene took Brian's hand. She had tears streaming down her face. Brian put an arm round his wife. As he did, he saw Wanda. She smiled at him. Brian smiled back. Holy fuck, when could he go?

But he was going nowhere as 'Hallelujah', the great Leonard Cohen song, hauntingly sung by one of the girl cousins pushed through the sadness and brought the crowd together.

Black hands joined white hands as 'Hallelujah' took David to a better place.

———

Sheila had asked Adrian if he'd like a lift to the funeral. She knew he was busy with some building work out bush somewhere and so she never expected him to say yes. But he did, and now they were sitting on a couple of dodgy chairs opposite from Wanda and Benny.

Thing about Adrian was he was full of surprises. Sheila found that sexy. She might get lucky when she dropped him home. Who knows? Or maybe Mr Nasty will be back by then.

Adrian was glad Sheila had asked if he wanted to go to the kid's funeral. He was keen for a break. Fella was busting his balls out bush and he was looking for an excuse. He'd never been to an Indigenous funeral before. Only real connection he'd had with Indigenous people was in the old days, at two-up. They called it Thommo's two-up school, but that name had stuck no matter who ran it. Changed places all the time. An empty block of ground in Paddo one night and a car park in Edgecliff the next. Back of Darling-hurst then down in Woolloomooloo. You never knew. Word just got around and the punters would turn up.

And a few of the punters were blackfellas. And the black-fellas always had Mumma Pearl with them. Looking out for them. Making sure they didn't get pissed and do all their dough.

Everyone respected Mumma Pearl. Everyone.

———

As 'Hallelujah' faded people turned to each other and hugged. Didn't matter they didn't know each other, just felt right.

One by one, friends and relatives came to the mike to talk about David.

'Beautiful smile.'

'Touched my heart.'

'Can't believe you gone, big fella.'

Very simple and very real and very sad.

A cousin, a Gumbaynggirr just as David was, sang to David the Gumbaynggirr Warrior.

Brian was amazed at how singing and music were such a natural part of the ceremony.

It always felt imposed or a little false at funerals he'd been to, but here it seemed natural. He wondered if maybe the blackfellas knew something about life and death that he didn't.

Nolene leant into him. She was in the zone. Brian thought maybe she had some blackfella in her. Wouldn't be surprised. Always going walkabout. Down to Melbourne or Sydney for meetings. Or up to Brisbane. Brian wondered when she might be going walkabout again.

Looking across at Wanda was making him horny. Fuck, cool down, mate, you're at a funeral.

And now Uncle Jack spoke. An Elder. He spoke of the Dreaming and of the spirit and how now David was with his ancestors. And into the sky flew white doves. Ten white doves one after the other. And finally, Gurrumul's voice rose out of the speakers searching for heaven. It was like he was standing there in his blindness singing for David.

Singing for the mourners. It can't get more beautiful. How can sad be so beautiful?

Moira stood in front of the microphone. Waited for Gurrumul to finish. Another life finished too soon. Moira knew his music would last forever. He'd been given time for his music.

Moira wondered what David might have achieved with more time.

'Thank you all for coming and farewelling my boy.'

Moira was grateful for the kind words that had been spoken.

Her words were private and would only be said to David.

'There's food and tea back home. Everyone is welcome.'

And then eight of the men in their black outfits and red bandanas lifted the coffin and placed it into the hearse.

Moira began to sing.

'Amazing grace, how sweet the sound,

'That saved a wretch like me.'

She was joined by the family around the mike.

'I once was lost, but now am found,

'Was blind but now can see.'

And then the mourners began repeating the verse.

No one noticed the fella at the back. He'd been there for the whole service. He reckoned he owed the kid that.

8

After the hearse moved off to the local cemetery, most mourners stayed on the island talking. Only family and close friends were invited to the burial.

It was mid-afternoon when everyone gathered at Moira's.

Sandwiches and tea must have been a turn-on cause Moira's house was packed. Not the full crowd of mourners but enough to fill the kitchen and lounge room and spill out into the backyard. Anything you could sit on outside was sat on. Chairs, benches, an upturned wheelbarrow, car tyres and garden tables. The mood was not solemn. It was the time to celebrate the life of a young blackfella who everyone had loved. Laughter went with hugs. Hugs went with handshakes. Trays carrying cups overflowing with tea were appearing through the open screen door at the rate of knots. Sandwiches were being gobbled up.

Sergeant Tommy Gallagher was the only whitey back at the house. He had tried to persuade a couple of David's schoolteachers to join him but they gave their apologies, saying they didn't want to crash something that was probably just for family.

The sergeant knew the house. They'd had a chat around the dining room table a few weeks back. Him, Moira and Wayne. Working out how to keep Wayne out of jail. Needing to get the bottle shop owner to go along with their plan. And happily for everyone he did. Decent bloke, the bottle shop owner.

As the afternoon slipped away and evening closed in, out came guitars and didgeridoos.

A barbecue was sparked up and bundles of snags found their way onto the hotplate.

By now there were about forty stayers. Music wound its way through all forty.

Things had quietened.

Mellow.

The sergeant sat on the wheelbarrow. Somehow a beer had ended up in his hand. He watched and listened. Wasn't going to learn anything about David's drowning. He knew that. But that bloody nag was there. Fucking thing. Wished it would piss off. Knew it wouldn't.

Not until it was satisfied.

David's bike. Where the fuck was it?

Head office didn't give a stuff. Waved it off.

'So the kid's bike is missing, Tommy, so what? One of his mates will have it or have sold it. You know what those blackfellas are like. What's yours is mine. Everyone owns everybody's everything.'

And then David's phone was a nag too. Tommy knew the kid had it at the beach, so how come no one had found it? They'd found David.

Head office had tracked David's number on the day before he was found. He'd been out bush during the afternoon and early evening but they couldn't pinpoint an exact location. Not enough towers to do that. And while the ridges weren't mountains, they did make reception difficult. So much for triangulation. Great when it works but bloody annoying when it doesn't. Tommy wasn't sure all this new technology amounted to much but DNA and CCTV had helped solve a stack of cases. Tommy and a couple of cops went out bush, but nothing. Needle in a gummy.

Night showed David to be by the beach, but again not exactly where.

No bike, no phone.

Just a nag.

———

Sarge wandered into the kitchen. Moira was washing cups and plates.

'Another beer, Sarge?'

'No thanks, Moira. Nice ceremony, don't you think?'

'Yep, David would have liked to have been there, that's for sure.'

Wayne wandered in. Caught the last bit.

'Yeah, hated attention, our David.'

They laughed.

Then silence. Lost in David.

'You want to see his room, Sarge?'

'Sure. Had a bit of a squiz after David was found but not a proper look. Ta.'

And Wayne and the sarge wandered down the hall to David's room.

'Don't you make a mess of it,' she called.

'Don't worry, Moira. Not gonna touch anything.'

The room was immaculate. Tidy as. Good for Moira. Her boy's bedroom.

There was a desk with schoolbooks. A window looked out into the yard. People eating at the barbie.

Comic books lay on his bed. Donald Duck. And hip stuff like Marvel.

Posters on the wall.

And the posters were all of cars. Classic Aussie cars.

A red Holden HZ Sandman panel van.

A yellow Holden VF Commodore.

A blue Holden FJ ute.

A Holden XU-1 Torana.

And in pride of place in the middle, on the biggest poster, an orange Holden HQ GTS Monaro with a black stripe down the bonnet.

'Loved that GTS. Reckoned one day he'd have one. Absolute classic, he reckoned.'

Sergeant Tommy Gallagher leant forward to take a good look at David's favourite car.

9

The Monaro had great upholstery. Leather. He'd been sitting in it since he drowned the boy. Working out what to do with him. She was downstairs, locked away. He'd finished with her. The voice was back. God, he hated that voice. Never properly went away. Always lurking.

'Shut that kid up. If you don't shut it up, I will.'

Been there from his first breath. That fucking voice. For thirty-fucking-seven years.

'Shut that kid up.'

And it was there now. But he'd learnt if he sat in the Monaro and took breaths then it would go. One, two, three, breathe in. One, two, three, breathe out. Relax.

And it was going.

Going.

Gone.

He would belt her sometimes, Dave would, if she couldn't make the baby shut up. That's what he was told to call him, right from the beginning. 'I'm not Dad, I'm not Pop, I'm Dave, remember that.'

Amazing how someone as fucking evil as he was could teach you anything. But truth was he did. Taught the fella everything he needed to know.

Dave knew how to wire up the house so the neighbours paid for the electricity. Fucking smart.

And the water. Understood plumbing. Got into the other neighbours' pipes. He paid for fuck all. And he made sure the fella was involved. Showed him everything. Taught him to drive nice and early too. Must've been only fourteen. Something like that. Needed someone to drive while he nicked stuff from building sites. In and out fast.

There had been a few family cars. All Holdens. He was a Holden man. But the prize was the Monaro. Dave loved it. Wouldn't scream at the Monaro. No. No way. It defined him. Powerful. Loud. He was so full of shit. It also fucked him.

The only time niceness happened was thanks to the Monaro. Stupid fucking word. 'Niceness.' But it was the only word to describe those times.

'Sunday-drive time, everyone. Into the Monaro. Make sure you wash your hands. Any mess on the upholstery and you'll pay for it.'

And he meant it and they washed their hands.

And they would drive for hours. Out west. Up and down the coast. And they'd stop for lunch at some country pub or beach cafe. It was different. Dave was different. They were like a proper family having a Sunday outing. And he was nice to everyone, saying please and thank you and laughing. He'd ask if the fella wanted an ice cream or he'd buy her some flowers.

When they got home he'd wash and clean the car forever. Inside and out. The prize Monaro.

The fella had turned eighteen when it happened. This Saturday morning she'd arrived back from the shops with Dave. She got out of the Monaro carrying bags of groceries and one bag broke and stuff fell out onto the back seat. A bottle of tomato sauce exploded. He came round.

'What the fuck have you done, you silly bitch?'

And then he whacked her around the head. Once, twice, three times. She fell to the ground screaming and then he kicked her in the head and blood came gushing. She had to go to hospital. She told the doctor who stitched her up that she fell and hit her head on the side of the car.

They were meant to be going for a drive the next day, but the fella knew they wouldn't be going. That night he loosened the two front wheel nuts.

Dave didn't get further than the telegraph pole at the end of the street. He loved to tear down the street. Let the neighbours hear his prize. But when the front wheels came off, all anybody heard was the Monaro slamming into the pole.

They burned him during the week. That's all they did, burned him. Cremation, they called it. No prayers, no tears. Just relief. The insurance paid for the repair of the Monaro. And now the fella had the Monaro. The family car. Wouldn't Dave love that. Not.

It was his and it was sitting in the shed. And he was sitting in it and working out what to do with the drowned kid. Stupid fucker. What the fuck was he doing sniffing around?

He knew he'd seen the girl. Seen him leading her up from the bunker. Buried beneath the house.

_____

'We're going to make you a cubby house,' Dave had said one morning during the school holidays. 'Like what Simmonds was trying to do.'

Simmonds and Newcombe were involved in one of Australia's greatest manhunts. It was during the late fifties. Dave loved the story. The pair of escapees had killed a prison officer and gone on the run. Five hundred cops, aeroplanes and helicopters, searched New South Wales looking for the pair. The cops were made to look like a bunch of bumbling dopes. Newcombe was apprehended after two weeks but Simmonds couldn't be found. Too smart. The public loved him. Another Ned Kelly. Australians love a crim, especially one who makes the cops look stupid. Eventually he was discovered digging a large hole in Ku-ring-gai Chase National Park, north of Sydney, attempting to hide a caravan. Simmonds had been free for five weeks.

It was all over the news. Radio was full of it. Usual bullshit. Talking to anyone who'd grown up with Simmonds. Didn't matter how well they knew him or didn't, they wanted their story.

Pictures of Simmonds on the front pages of the newspapers for days. Pictures of the hole and the caravan. Fuck-all about Newcombe. The forgotten escapee, they called him.

Dave had grown up with the story. Was only eight at the time but no kid could escape it. All the kids wanted to be Simmonds. Played 'escaping the cop' games at school. You wouldn't have wanted to be one of the cops. Look like a fuckwit. Had to be a baddie.

And now here he was in his forties telling the fella

they were going to do what Simmonds tried to do. Dig a hole and bury a caravan in it. Make a cubby house. Underground.

And they did. Dug a bloody great hole. Huge. Yep, big enough for a caravan. But where to get the caravan?

'Don't you worry about that little problem. I'll find one.'

And he did. It was a couple of streets away. And it was the middle of the night. Caravan was out on the street. Dave backed the car up. Hitched the caravan onto it and drove off. Then drove up the side of their house. Round the back. Unhitched. And threw a tarp over it.

Next day there was a bit of a furore around the place. A caravan had been nicked. Door knocking.

'Had my caravan knocked off last night. You haven't seen anything, have you?'

'No, mate, but I'll keep an eye out. Some people will thieve anything, won't they? No scruples.'

And then back to the 'bloody great hole'.

They got it in there. Took a few days. Ropes and pulleys.

Neighbours didn't notice. Everyone was banging and sawing in their backyards in those days. Building sheds. And anyway, the caravan was covered until it was dropped in the hole and the tarp thrown back over.

But then the work really started. The electrics. The plumbing. Putting in a toilet.

Now the fella was really learning. Not just nicking water and electricity from the neighbours but wiring up and welding and laying pipes.

And Dave was a perfectionist. Got to get it right. No use doing it half-hearted.

If you did it half-hearted, then a blow to the back of the head was a given.

When he built his own cubby which now had a lodger, girl lodger, he felt he was reliving those days back home with him and her.

Being belted by him and comforted by her. But very little comforting, because if Dave saw comforting it would be another blow to the head.

'What are you? A mummy's boy.' Whack. And then down below.

'Don't put him down there again. It's no good for his health. It's got mould.'

Then a whack for her and a hand to the back of the neck for him and down into the cubby he was steered. Door shut. Silence.

———

After the Monaro steering wheel went through his neck, she started to fade. It was as though she was there to look out for the fella and take the shit that poured out of Dave.

Not that she could do much. It must have taken every bit of strength to hang in there, and so when the cunt died she gave in.

He didn't have much time with her. He didn't really know what to do. He sat by her hospital bed and looked at her. Who was she?

She'd been scared all the time that he'd known her. From his birth until now. Eighteen years. Was she scared before he was born? Had to be. That's how Dave ruled. With fear. What was their life before him? Was it ever like in the movies?

'I love you.'

'I love you too.'

And they'd kiss.

He'd never seen a kiss. Movies must be bullshit.

———

He got the house and the Monaro and stayed. No point going anywhere. Apprenticed to a carpenter and an electrician to get his certificate. Didn't learn much. Truth was he knew more than they taught him. Knew all the illegal twists and turns too. Finally the authorities got onto him about the electrics and plumbing and stealing from next door. Told them he knew nothing about it. That it had to have been Dave. They fined him and made him pay the arrears from when he took over ownership of his home. Home. That was a laugh. Nothing homey about that house.

———

John Laws, the king of the airwaves, talked about an All Holden Day car show. The fella loved Lawsy, and if Lawsy said it would be a great day then he and the Monaro were going. So the Monaro went for a run. Been doing a lot of runs. Ever since Dave. Fuck Dave.

He loved it. Had people ogling the Monaro and congratulating him on what a great beast it was and what great condition the beast was in.

More shows followed. Got offered a fair bit of coin for the beast, but no way it was for sale. Ever.

At a show up the coast he got talking to a bloke called Adrian. Adrian was very taken by the Monaro.

'Love your beast, mate. How long you had it?'

And that's how it started. Talked cars and engines. Shared a couple of beers. The fella said he lived down Newcastle way. About a hundred k's north of it, to be precise. Adrian said how he loved being out of cities and on the coast. Spoke about the beaches and The Basin. The fella listened.

And that's how he ended up selling 'the family home' and buying his twenty acres up the coast.

And now was sitting in the Monaro with a dead kid on the ground outside and a young woman locked down in the bunker.

10

She was not going to die down here in this bunker. He
hobbled her like with prisoners in movies. A clasp on either
ankle joined by a chain. He asked her how she was. She
screamed at him. He ignored her. He would check on her
daily. Bring food. She asked him what he wanted from
her but he wouldn't answer.

A few days in, she found out. It must have been night.
Felt like night. There were two doors to the bunker. One
was a steel grilled prison-like door facing into the bunker
and behind it a heavy wooden door. He opened the wooden
door and stood staring at her then he told her to sit on the
bed. She did as he said, then he opened the grilled door and
entered. He unshackled her.

'Lie down.'

And she did.

She wanted to live.

She was not going to die down here in this bunker.

This would be over soon. Even though there would be
other times. She knew that.

Then he came over to her. Took off his shirt and lay on top of her.

'Put your arms around me.'

And she did.

She heard him whisper something. And again. She strained to hear.

And there it was.

'Mummy.'

He stayed like that. Just lay on top of her. Leila didn't know for how long. And then he got up, put his shirt on. He picked up the manacles.

'We won't need these anymore, will we?'

Then he left and closed the doors to the bunker.

Leila lay still on the mattress, staring at the door, wondering what had just happened.

This became a ritual.

'Mummy.'

Leila asked for a clock. She begged him. Just to know what part of the day she was in. There was only artificial light in the bunker, from lamps set into the wall, controlled from where she had no idea.

He said he'd think about a clock. Maybe. Would depend on her behaviour. Leila promised to behave.

Leila went back through it in her mind. She didn't remember how she had come into the bunker. Woke from a sleep and there she was.

Demanded her mind to come out of the fog. The Basin. Working. The party for Conchita. Finishing work. Dancing and drinking. Drinking too much. Swimming?

Walking home. Alone.

A van.

And then it got foggy.

Opening the door to her flat.

An arm around her waist.

A rag over her nose and mouth.

And then the bunker. Fuck. Fuck. Fuck. And no one can hear. Where the fuck was she?

The next time he came in, he gave her a clock. He had wrapped it in fancy paper. Like a present. She thanked him.

When he left, she unwrapped the clock. It was an old wind-up clock with a round face. She remembered the type from her childhood. Leila held the clock in her hands. Then to her chest. A small step. A small step forward for now.

———

Leila grew up in Copenhagen. Snowboarded throughout Scandinavia but a bad fall in Norway had led to a broken back. It was a bad break. She was in hospital for a month then in a brace for twelve weeks. Rehab for another twelve weeks. The doctors thought Leila would be okay but the pain persisted, and so she had surgery. Fusion of two vertebrae.

She had never known depression or anxiety. She needed help. A psychologist and medication came to the rescue. Eventually she healed. Learnt you can get through anything. It's a mind game. Small steps.

Leila's mum loved movies and had seen a number of Australian films from the eighties. Films that showed great distances covered with red soil and the odd small town. The 'outback', it was called. She played them for Leila during her rehabilitation.

Leila decided she was going to Australia.

There was no great distance or red soil or small town where she was now. Only a concrete room with a bed, a pot for the toilet and a bucket of water and a towel.

Leila had read up on Australia. Hot and sunny and big. The opposite of Denmark. And Leila wanted something very different from the life she knew. She wanted to test herself. Test the new Leila. The Leila who struggled through a year of pain and rehab and didn't go under. She knew she was a different person. A stronger person. How strong, she had to find out. Maybe on the other side of the world where she knew no one. So she bought a ticket. She was going to find out.

Leila made a pact with her mum and dad. She would text them how she was going at the beginning of every month. Absolutely on the first day of the month. That was the plan. They were worried. Didn't like that.

'What if you are in trouble? We won't know. What if you're stranded in the outback and need money?'

'That's why I'm going, to handle things on my own. Please trust me, I'll be fine. I know I will.'

They had no choice. She was a hard head, their Leila. Always was, and since the accident harder than ever. But if she said first of the month then that's what they could look forward to.

Six weeks later they tearfully hugged their daughter goodbye at Copenhagen airport. It would be weeks before her first text. Wrong. It was less than five hours.

what the hell am I going to do here in Frankfurt airport for thirteen hours.
. . . it's boring having a thirteen-hour layover . . miss you.

But that was the last text until the first of the coming month. Three weeks away.

Leila knew she was going to the other side of the world. It took so fucking long. Forty-three hours before she set foot in Brisbane Australia. There was a further layover of seven hours in Singapore. Sure she could have taken a quicker flight with shorter layovers but that would have meant a higher price. Nope, she was saving money. Money was limited time was not.

———

Leila spent one night at a backpackers' hostel in Brisbane before setting off for Byron Bay, a skip across the border into northern New South Wales. Byron Bay was known worldwide by backpackers. Sun and surf and romance and fun, fun, fun. And Leila was up for it all before stage two, which was red soil and the Dead Heart. No beaches or surf or romance there. Well, maybe romance. That can be found in the weirdest places.

Leila knew about romance. She had been in love. Deeply in love. With Frederick. Older and wiser and married. Who of course was going to leave his wife for Leila.

It was Frederick who had organised the snowboarding holiday. Yes, the one where Leila broke her back. This was the holiday he'd said they'd have before he told his wife about her. He had told his wife he had a business deal to finalise in Norway. Needed to be there or the deal might fall apart.

It wasn't the deal that fell apart, it was the romance. Broken back. Broken heart. Frederick stuck around for a day to make sure she wasn't dead. What a guy. And then explained that maybe this was a sign that the romance was doomed. That with his business he didn't have the time to be a carer. And then he was off. The fucker.

Wow, you can be lucky. How many more years would Frederick have used her as his *elskerinde* or as the English say, 'piece on the side'? Thank god for the accident. Got a lot out of that accident.

So now her slate was clean and Leila was ready to fill it in. Come on, adventure. Come on, life.

Leila was ready for whatever that was.

11

The New South Wales coastline is something else. Headland. Beach. Headland. Beach. Big beaches ten or fifteen kilometres long or small hidden beaches nestled into the rocks and maybe only a hundred metres long. Blue, blue ocean with white or golden-white sand and surf peeling off white water. And mostly empty of people.

But not Byron. There were plenty of people in Byron.

Back in the day, banana plantations and acres of market gardens nurturing every vegetable under the sun kept Byron humming.

And then in the sixties and seventies the joint was discovered by alternate lifestylers.

And joint was the word. Roll 'em and smoke 'em. Good weed in those tropical hills.

Yep indeedy, Byron was a hippie hangout. It was also loved by the boardies.

That was the new game in town in the sixties. Australia discovered surfing. Swapped speedos for baggies. Baggies that of course hung down to your knees and had mostly Hawaiian prints. Or maybe just yellow or blue or anything, as long as they were baggies hanging deep.

Midget Farrelly the dancer. Nat Young the animal. Bob McTavish the innovator and Peter Drouyn the explorer. And many other greats, spewed out of long, beautiful tubes. And they were champions, those boys. Won world championships. Won at Sunset beating the Yanks.

On the nose or hanging five. And The Beach Boys grooving that the only thing that meant anything was 'Surfin' USA'.

Surf and weed and music. Plenty of all three. And then festivals. The Blues Festival and the Falls Festival. And the same vibe still lives on in Byron today. With lots more people and much more expensive weed. And pills. No longer the sixties. Progressed just as the drugs had.

Leila floated out of the bus. The hostel was in the centre of town.

She could feel the vibe.

She loved it. She needed it.

———

The hostel was easy as. A room to yourself and a five-minute stroll to the beach.

Leila couldn't get over the difference from home. Everyone almost nude. Almost. Girls in what passed for a bikini and boys tanned and muscular. At home they'd all be rugged up in parkas and scarves and long underwear under jeans. And thick caps.

Got to keep the head warm. No skin to be seen until hot-bath time inside a heated house.

Not in Byron. Skin everywhere. Leila knew she'd melt into the crowd after a couple of days of sun and in a new string bikini. And she did and she knew she looked great. A tanned Scandi.

A hot tanned Scandi.

Within a week she had a bunch of friends and a job. Waitressing at a cool restaurant, Legs. Yep, they liked it if you showed them but no hassle if you didn't but why wouldn't you? Hot jeans and long dresses made no sense.

Her hours were great. Two in the arvo until ten pm. How come these Australians shorten every word they can? Meant a laze on the beach, chatting, swimming and choosing.

'I bags him.'

'No, I want him. You can have that one.'

'But I saw him first. Fuck off. Find your own.'

And they'd laugh and tease and be alive.

And the after-work partying at a bar on the beach. Leila could feel her mind and body losing all heaviness.

'Too much for the human unit,' her friend Ryan would say. Didn't take him long to drop into 'Aussie'. Doesn't take anyone long to drop into Aussie at Byron.

Ryan was from Paris and on a year's break after graduating as a doctor from the Sorbonne.

Leila pulled him out of the surf at Byron. It wasn't a particularly big day but if you don't know rips you can get into plenty of trouble. And Ryan didn't know rips. He was flapping around too scared to yell for help when Leila noticed him. She swam to him and told him to relax. That she would help him to shore. Ryan was very pleased when they hit the sand. Kissed it.

'Wow, I really love sand.'

Leila laughed and from that moment they were friends.

———

Ryan's 'great-great-great-whatever' had been a doctor to the King of Persia. Ryan was very proud of that and proud of the fact that for as far back as he knew there had always been a doctor in his family. Being a doctor wasn't just about fixing bodies, it was a vocation. A purpose. A commitment to the advancement of the human species. That's how Ryan's family saw it. Leila loved Ryan's passion.

Time passed. First of the month:

hi mum dad in a place called byron bay look it up paradise you'd love it
feel great and lovely new friends no need to worry not sure what plans
red soil might have to wait

Love you miss you hope all good at home xxxxxxxxxxxxxxxx

The return text was rather longer, updating Leila on goings-on in Copenhagen with friends and family. Her mum and dad were pleased she was so happy but of course told her to be careful.

And Leila was careful. She was no idiot. Things can happen. Bad things. Very bad things.

And so can wonderful things. That was what she had learnt during her rehab and fighting her anxiety and depression.

She knew the answer wasn't hiding away. Keeping her life small. That's what the voices suggested. No, no hiding. Fear and avoidance were killers. She'd learnt to end those conversations.

———

Days passed. New friends were made. Every new friend was like a friend for life or like you'd known them all your life. What is that? Is that what the secret of travelling is when you are young, sharing new experiences? Telling your story. Revealing your loves, your vulnerabilities, without fear.

Is it the anonymity?

If it is the anonymity, then are all the stories true? Probably not. Does it matter? And there you are. Stuff like that to think about. What fucking fun. Leila was alive.

Ryan went to Sydney. They had become close. Not romantically. But Leila knew Ryan cared about her just as Leila cared about him. She hoped they might be friends for life.

She gave him her phone number and her parents' number in Copenhagen.

'Keep in touch, Ryan.'

'I will.'

'Promise?'

'Promise.'

And they hugged and stepped back from each other and laughed. Friends.

———

It was a beautiful Byron day. Leila realised that was the only description for the day. Simple.

Life is often that simple. It's just you don't see it. You complicate it. Leila was not into complicating anything today.

She had decided during the week that time was up in Byron. Didn't mean she wouldn't be back, but the adventure was on the move.

It was move-on day.

Goodbyes were said the night before. The restaurant turned on a party after closing. Singing and dancing and all sorts of good bullshit.

And don't the Australians love the word bullshit. They use it in so many different ways. There's good bullshit and bad bullshit. It was rubbing off. Leila would now search for more bullshit down the coast.

12

Anna was beautiful. That's what all the boys told her. She liked the boys telling her she was beautiful but she also knew why they told her. They wanted some of the forbidden fruit. The nuns had talked about the forbidden fruit that Eve offered to Adam. That's why the world was getting more fucked up all the time, because way back Adam took the forbidden fruit. The nuns said the forbidden fruit was an apple. Anna thought it was dumb to make an apple the forbidden fruit. An apple wasn't at all sexy. It should have been a peach, Anna believed. A mushy sexy peach.

Manuel wants some of Anna's sexy peach but there is no way. No way in hell. Which is where Manuel should end up. No question. In hell.

Manuel is the latest in a long line of boyfriends. Not for Anna. For her mother. And her mother has had babies with the whole line. Anna's dad was the first and that was eighteen years ago.

Manuel is becoming a pest. A drunken, fondling pest. So far Anna has been able to keep him at bay but it is getting very uncomfortable. Her mother, Maria, missed most of the uncomfortable moments because Manuel was usually passed out on the lounge when she returned from work.

Anna is from São Carlos, a small city some two hundred and fifty kilometres from São Paulo, the biggest city in South America.

Anna loves her country. Her Brazil. She loves being a Brazilian girl. She loves the festivals, the music, the vitality that lives in her Brazil. But life is becoming very hard for people like Anna. Poor people. God, she hates saying that. Poor. Anna is not a victim and will never be a victim but she needs a change. She wants to live like the Brazilian men and women who walk Oscar Freire in São Paulo and purchase from the shops bearing the designer labels. Cartier. Gucci. Chanel. Dior.

Last year Anna travelled to São Paulo for the Gay Pride Parade. The biggest Gay Pride Parade in the world outside of New York. She loved it. Loved the parade and loved São Paulo and loved the malls and the churches and the skyscrapers. She loved how the city lights glowed in the big, mirrored skyscrapers. The tallest skyscrapers in the Southern Hemisphere.

And Anna loves the Latin motto that defines São Paulo. *Non ducor, duco*. I am not led, I lead.

That is what Anna will do. She will lead. One day.

Anna's mother works as a maid. Long hours for little money and although their house is small, with just two bedrooms, the rent is high and each day the price of food seems to rise. There is little joy to be had.

Working on reception at a car hire company allows Anna to meet people from other worlds. Worlds she escapes into. She studied hard at school to learn English because that's what you need to speak to forge ahead in this capitalist world. Anna isn't fluent in English but she knows how to make herself understood. She knows she is an asset to the company with her good looks and outgoing personality. Customers enjoy talking to her.

José sure does. He is a customer and a real gentleman. Often takes a car. Never comes onto her like so many customers. He is cool is José.

13

Meeting Adrian at the car show was the push the fella needed to sell up and move. Put the place in the hands of an agent, and whoopee, a handful of bickies came his way. Bloody lot of handfuls. Bloody lot of bickies.

He hadn't mentioned to the agent about the cubby in the ground. No one would have a clue what was down there. Grown over. But one day someone was going to put a shovel into the ground and strike a caravan and then they were going to open it up and then they'd find the Vegemite jar, with his ashes in it. Whoever found it would reckon the Vegemite looked like shit. Because that was where he was laid to rest.

It was her idea.

'Now cover the thing over and plant some grass.'

And he did.

——

The twenty acres was a fair way out the back. It was a good half-hour's drive to the popular old pub where Slim

Dusty sang in the good old days and then you kept going for another twenty minutes straight to the end of the valley, where there was a dirt road for another ten minutes with about five private driveways all with gates bolted and signs declaring you were dead if you even thought about entering. David had found out they meant it.

The fella told the real estate agent, Brian-something, that he wanted privacy. So privacy was what he was shown. Agent had listened.

His was the last gate. Pretty forestry all round. Isolated.

The twenty acres had a couple of buildings. A house of sorts—the shack. Two bedrooms. Shower and shithouse. And a decent-sized kitchen with room for a table six could sit around. There weren't ever going to be six sitting around it. He knew that for sure. No visitors. No unwanted visitors. No intruders.

It was perfect, as was the price, even with dodgy wi-fi and lousy phone reception. Wi-fi was from a satellite. Australia was supposed to be the lucky country with plenty of dosh to spread about, but try and get good wi-fi or phone reception and you'd think you were out the back of one of those African countries. And you know they probably had it running good there. Still, he didn't really mind. More private.

Seemed the previous owners only had it two years. Vietnamese. Tried growing tomatoes. Must have failed, otherwise why sell?

There was a shed that could look after the Monaro. Needed a bit of fixing up as did everything but some sheets of gal and a little woodwork would sharpen it up. There was a small dam near the shed and a water tank taking runoff from the house.

A tractor was tossed in with the price. About ten years old. It would get plenty of use.

He'd known straight away that this was the right place. He could be happy here. It had everything. Except for one thing. And that he'd have to build.

There were plenty of trees on the property so no need to go buy wood. He had all the tools. After all, he was a qualified carpenter and electrician. Very fucking qualified. No flies on him. He'd set up his own timber mill.

He wanted to build under the house so he would need to brace the house which was on wooden bearings. And he'd be doing it on his own. It would be done on the quiet. On the real quiet because it had a purpose and no one was going to know about the bunker and its purpose.

He told the agent to sort it out. Bargained a bit. Got them down twenty grand. Exchanged fast, since he had the money. Didn't need finance. Brian-something sorted it out. Fast. He was good.

It was on an early morning recce when he discovered the weed. About twenty plants. Good size. Healthy with some nice thick heads. Bloke who'd owned it must have forgotten or else he was passing on a crop as a gift to the new owner. Stranger things have happened. He had built a sort of long cage with chicken wire to keep the kangas away. The crop was only some ten metres from his fence-line into the state forest. That's what the local small-timers did and even the big-timers at times. No culpability if the plants were spotted by the cops.

'No idea, sir. Never go into the forest. Scary. Never know what's in there. Goannas as big as crocs. No, sir, too scary for me.'

Or some such bullshit.

The past owner, or whoever, had to have been watering the plants because they were in too good a nick. Would've been rude not to check out the produce. Bloody rude. So he'd gone straight back to the house and rolled a big one. Very nice. Very, very nice indeed. He was incredibly grateful and very stoned.

He kept an eye on the crop just in case it belonged to a big bad boy. And he knew the big bad boys were definitely very bad. But none came by, so he helped himself whenever.

Life was looking pretty good now. He had the Monaro. That cunt of a father was dead. His mum wasn't getting belted anymore. The family home with its evil was no longer around. And now his own little plantation in arm's reach.

It was nice to know that after a hard day's building there would be a little something to smoke in the cool of the evening and the fading pink light of the day.

———

Adrian had finished a surf. Two-metre swell and offshore. It was one of those days. You can't describe them. Just one of those days. He'd been in the water for over two hours. Felt fit. Thought a coffee was in order, so hello The Basin.

Adrian had mentioned The Basin to the fella with the Monaro so wasn't all that surprised to see him drinking a coffee there. He was sitting at the table in the sun. It was the only table in the sun. Most blokes were a bit over sun these days. Had too much skin burnt off over the years. Gotta be careful of the melanomas. Hats and sun block now and even caps when surfing. Except for the bald blokes, who never wore anything on their skulls. Adrian couldn't work that one out.

'Fancy seeing you here.'

'Yeah.'

'On your way to another classic car show?'

'No.'

'What you doing here then? Long way from Newcastle to come for coffee.'

'Bought a few acres out the back.'

'No.'

'Yep, you sold the area pretty good. Looked around. Found something.'

And that was how Adrian's association with the fella with the Monaro had started.

Fella didn't come in every day but you might see him a couple of times in the month.

He was flat out he told Adrian. The old shack he'd bought needed quite a bit of work done on it. But that was okay because he was up for it. Liked working with his hands.

He never did say exactly where it was. Just out the back. You learnt not to be nosy. Not that anyone was necessarily hiding anything, but people had come up the coast to get away. So you kept the questions general.

'Your van?'

'Yep.'

'Where's the beast?'

'Locked up.'

'You ever need an extra pair of hands, give me a yell. Here's my number. Twenty-five bucks an hour.' Adrian wrote out his number on a napkin and handed it to the fella.

'Ta.'

Fella put it in his wallet but didn't hand over his number.

'Better get a move on. Plenty to do.'

And then he shook Adrian's hand and headed to his van.

'See you round.'

Adrian watched the fella drive off. Strange fucker, he thought. But that's okay, just another strange fucker up the coast.

———

It was almost three weeks later that Adrian saw the fella again. Adrian was having a morning surf at the three-kilometre mark. There were three of them out. Benny and Ken had beaten him by a half hour. Very pleasant one-metre mal waves. They shared.

Eventually Benny went in. Didn't want to but the shop called. Then Ken called it a morning. He would be back later. An evening surf.

When Adrian finished and wandered towards his van there was the fella sitting on a small sandhill. He had a smoke in his hand.

Adrian sat down.

'Looks nice out there,' the fella said. 'Wish I surfed.'

'Never too late. Is that what I think it is?'

'Want a hit?' And the fella handed the joint to Adrian. Adrian took a blast.

'Not bad. Yours?'

The fella said nothing but gave a slight grin.

'You got more of that, I can find you a few customers. Nothing big but there's plenty round here like the odd smoke . . . if it's good stuff. And this is pretty good. Nice and easy.'

'I've got your number. I'll give you a ring.'

And then the fella was off.

Adrian felt rather great. Thought he'd go back for another wave now he had a contact.

14

The bus ride was okay. Nothing to write home about. The new freeway meant you saw a fair dose of green and then every hour or so a town. Leila wasn't sure where she was going. Just going with the flow. As the current dictated.

One of the little towns would give out a signal. 'Out here, out here,' it would call. Something like that. Leila smiled at her meanderings. She'd know when to get off or she'd be bored with the bus ride and just jump ship. She smiled to herself. Jump *bus*, you idiot.

Which is what she did. She was about four hours into the trip and stopped at a little town. Little quiet town on a river that ran into the sea. They all did. Leila knew the beaches couldn't be too far away.

The pub was on the river. A few locals having a beer on the veranda. The bloke behind the bar gave Leila a key for a room. It was upstairs and the bedroom door opened out onto another veranda looking down onto the river. Pretty nice for a Danish backpacker.

———

A salad on the veranda and a cold beer and Leila was ready to explore. She'd started to develop a liking for beer. Hardly drank it in Copenhagen. Every moment was a new adventure for Leila. She had decided that. It was her mantra.

The town was small with a couple of parallel streets running off what used to be the old highway. One of the streets ran along the river. Pretty. A lane took her through to the other street. The lane was covered in murals. Some definitely by an Indigenous artist. Whales and faces. Another showed the pub where she was staying, and a beach with surfers and another pub that must have been out of town.

'I will make some new friends and have a drink of beer at that pub soon,' Leila decided.

There was a coffee shop called Conchita's at the top of the lane. No try, no get. Another mantra.

'Hi.'

'Hi.'

'Lovely town you have here.'

'Glad you think so.' Conchita—it must have been Conchita, with her black curly hair—smiled.

'I'm looking for a job.'

'Couple of days late, I'm afraid, darling. I just brought on a new girl.'

'Oh, that's bad luck. Blast.'

'However I do know they're always looking for someone at The Basin, out at the beach. Try them.'

Conchita explained that the beach was only fifteen minutes away and that a bus went back and forth every hour on the hour.

Leila paid for a coffee and stayed chatting with Conchita until the bus arrived.

15

The fella rang Adrian. They arranged to meet at The Basin. Have a coffee.

'Bring your togs,' said Adrian. 'Have a swim, water's beautiful. I'll be catching a couple of waves before you get here.'

Not on your life was the fella going for a swim. He liked looking at the ocean and watching the surfers, but no chance he was going in there, where there were sharks. Was Adrian fucking joking? He reckoned they were all mad.

One day. One day a big, big bastard was going to come along with its mouth wide open. Its teeth screaming, 'I'm gonna fuckin' eat ya.' Its eyes sparkling with excitement. And snap. You were in half, with red, red blood, your blood, surging into that beautiful blue ocean. No way.

Nope. Sit on the beach and smoke a dooby. Much safer.

He'd been chainsawing logs for most of the morning. Bloody hard work. A drive to the beach and a coffee was what he needed.

Adrian was at the outside table with a coffee and cake when he arrived. Parked the van and joined him. They weren't the only ones at tables.

He ordered the same as Adrian and then passed him a paper bag full of heads.

'What d'you reckon this'd be worth?'

Adrian looked in the bag then took a sniff.

'About two-fifty.'

'Sounds good.'

Adrian told him that if he could supply five bags a week then he reckoned there would be a market.

'Yep, reckon I could do that. What do you want out of it?'

'I don't intend to sell it but I know a bloke who might. Let me talk to him. He'll want it at half that price so he can offload it at two-fifty. Me, I want just enough for the odd joint. I'm not greedy.'

They finished their coffees just as the local bus pulled up. Couple of people got off. A young woman and an old bloke, trying to navigate past about twenty schoolkids who were keen to get on and get home.

Adrian told him to get in touch in a few days and hopefully things would be sorted. He said he was cool with that.

As he got into his van he noticed the young woman who'd got off the bus heading into The Basin. She was pretty, he thought. He watched her.

———

He'd found a small excavator on the web. Well used, but still had a few miles left on the clock. Cost him twenty-five hundred plus a further five hundred to hire a truck to drive it to his place. He drove the truck himself. Didn't want anyone sniffing around.

He pretty much knew how he'd go about building the bunker. It was to go under the house with an entrance via a stairway at the side of the house.

He could have ripped up floorboards and started digging, removing the soil by bucket, but that was going to be murder on him and take forever so the answer was to use an excavator and dig from outside. Bracing the house properly was bloody important. Didn't want the thing collapsing down the hole.

There was plenty of forest and so plenty of wood to choose from. Flooded gums were everywhere but it was hardwood he wanted. And it was there among the gummies. Tallowwood and ironbark. Two of the many eucalypts on the property. He knew which wood he wanted but wasn't used to seeing it in a tree, covered in bark and with limbs and leaves. Google it. Always the answer now. Google. Dave used to have books around to find out stuff. *Encyclopedia Britannica*. A bloke had come to the house selling it. You got to pay it off over eighteen months.

He sat for a while looking at the forest. It was something he'd never done before. Wood was used to make stuff, not to look at. He found it calming.

Then he cleared an area to set up his mill and cut a couple of big stumps to sit his logs on.

Didn't muck around. He felled two big ones on the first

day and cut several posts using a chainsaw. Then an electric plane to dress the planks.

This was what he liked.

Back when, he would head out into the yard and work like crazy to get the sounds of the bashing out of his head. They should have been long gone but that's not how it works. They're there, biding their time, waiting to fuck with you.

He reckoned they wouldn't be fucking with him for some time. This bunker would take at least a month to finish.

The first week was slow going. He used the tractor to cart the logs and planks to the house. Logs the height of the bunker were placed under bearers to support the building, enabling the excavator to do its job. Bloody good buy, the excavator. He hated to think how long it would have taken by shovel.

And it was a shovel Dave had used to build a hole for the caravan. He was a strong bastard, that's for sure. Couldn't think about the pain she'd have experienced from that strong an arm.

He'd done bugger all with the house. It could wait until the bunker was finished then he'd start on it. But he did attend to the shed, after all that was the crib for the beast. Nothing must happen to the beast.

New sheets of gal and some planks sorted the shed out.

———

There had been a number of trips to the co-op for materials. Bloke asked him if he wanted to set up an account. Not a chance. He'd have had to supply them with an address and other details and that was never going to happen.

Co-op was a funny place. People nodded at you while you were getting your stuff. Nodded at you in a sort of knowing way like you belonged to the same tribe. Didn't matter if you were one of the old farmers from the area or a new farmer or a hippie from out back or a bikie or even one of those sheilas who were always wearing overalls and had their feet firmly planted in Blunnies. Same tribe. Same nod.

After a couple of weeks and four or five trips you started to recognise some of them. A bikie who'd been in a few times stopped him one morning. Scary-looking bastard with tatts and bikie jacket.

'How you going?'

'Yeah, good. Good. Yeah. You?'

Last thing he wanted was a conversation.

'Getting plenty of stuff. Must know your way around the building game. Builder, are you?'

He didn't want this but it was a fucking bikie and he'd better be civil. They're scary some of them bikies.

'No, but know enough.'

'You know electrics too?'

'Yep, know enough.'

'Need a bloke to fix a few leaks and shit. How you placed? Cash. No need for the taxman to know. Pay really well.'

Last thing he wanted to do. He nearly shat himself. But it was a bikie. What happens if he says no to a bikie? Slashed tyres? Bullet through the windscreen? Fucking paranoia. Fucking with his head.

Took a breath.

'You okay?'

'Yeah yeah, sorry, just a bit tired. Working my arse off.'

'So what do you say?'

He pulled himself together. Thought about it.

He wasn't exactly rolling in it. Buying the property took a heap. Sure, he wasn't broke but he would need to fill up the tank sometime. Shit. Shit. Shit.

'Oh yeah, could probably help you out.'

'Tomorrow?'

'Yeah, okay, tomorrow.'

The bikie gave him the address. It was out his way, only about ten k's away from the fella's property.

'See you tomorrow then. I'm Ace. You?'

Fuck! He didn't want to give his name to the bikie. What would be next? His address and then what, have him pop in for a beer?

'GT.'

'GT? GT? You kidding me?'

'That's what they call me.'

'Okay, GT. Tomorrow.'

'Yep, tomorrow.'

'Don't let me down.'

The bikie left the co-op and climbed into a big modern four-wheel parked out front. Looked back at the fella and then drove off.

———

Shit. Shit. Shit.

On the drive home in the van he took his breaths.

Convinced himself that it was a good move. The money would be handy. No ties. Only being a handyman, for fuck's sake. And that's how it started. Him working on and off for Ace the bikie, while finishing his bunker.

At home he went straight for the weed and rolled one. He took a big inhale. That was better.

Felt good.

Tomorrow would be another day. A good day. He knew that.

16

José mentioned to Anna that on the weekend he was driving to São Paulo for Fashion Week. Anna was so envious and she told José. Also told him she was not working this weekend. Did she tell José just to get an invite? Of course she did. How forward, she thought. And José obliged. But not before explaining that he was uncomfortable giving a young woman a lift to another city. He told her that she would need to have her own accommodation for the weekend. That there was no way he could help out there. She told him she had family in São Paulo and that she'd only need the lift.

'Not a problem, then.'

José was definitely cool.

José was definitely a gentleman.

Anna stayed with her family in São Paulo at night, but the two days were spent with José.

He knew people. He had invites to the fashion shows and introduced her to classy people. They were the people that Anna wanted to be like. Anna told José her thoughts.

Her dreams. Her desires. José showed her pictures of a place far from Brazil. A place called Australia. She had heard of it but knew nothing about it. The photos showed young men and women at bars and restaurants and at beaches and in the snow and riding horses through the desert and much, much more. Anna thought it a wonderful place. And it too was in the Southern Hemisphere. A warm place. Anna liked warmth. Brazil had warmth.

José told her many young South American women like her were there working. They worked on farms picking fruit and were earning so much money they didn't know what to spend it on. Money like engineers earn in Brazil. Money that they sent back to their families. Anna asked José how she might travel to Australia to work. He told Anna he might be able to arrange it, that he had a cousin in the migration business who helped Brazilians get a visa and find work for them when they arrived. It wasn't easy but if he could do it for Anna she would need to find a lot of money. Anna didn't have a lot of money, nor did she know how to get a lot of money. José knew how to get money. He could help. It would be a debt but one she would easily pay back with her Australian earnings. Anna was so happy. She hugged José and thanked him. She told José to arrange it while she would apply for a passport.

———

On the drive back to São Carlos, Anna dreamed. She saw herself in Australia picking fruit. Being paid handfuls of dollars. Swimming and laughing. Even skiing. Anna had never seen real snow but she would in Australia. What a place. A paradise.

Her mother cried when she heard of Anna's plans. She worried. Wanted to know who this José was. Manuel knew who José was. A peach picker. But Anna explained it would be helpful to the family. That her mother wouldn't have to work so hard. Her siblings could get some new clothes. Not have to wear second-hand clothes. That it would be only for a couple of years. Three at the most. Trust her. She knew what she was doing.

The next day Anna took her birth certificate to the passport office. They took a photo. Anna liked the photo. She looked pretty with her dark olive eyes, dark tanned skin, long hair and plump lips. This was the most exciting day of Anna's life.

Waiting for her passport to arrive meant Anna could learn more about Australia. Social media was filled with South Americans in Australia particularly Brazilian men surfing. She could hardly sleep with anticipation. There were bad experiences, of course. That happens everywhere. Anna knew how to look after herself. She was no baby.

17

mum dad. hello hello. out of byron now and futher down the coast
towards sydney another paradise I think maybe a little slower but
I know I will like it have job waitressing at the basin its called google
it .. all safe and miss you but good really good hope all okay at home
love L xxxx

There is nothing more laidback than early morning by the
beach. Leila was fully seduced by it. Shorts, thongs, hair
pulled back wet from a swim. Surfers walking to or from
the ocean. Locals reading the papers over a coffee. A couple
strolling the length of the beach for morning exercise. A little
exaggerated that. Didn't ever look like exercise. A 'hello', a
'good day'. And the light. Early morning light playing with
the sand and the blue.

The Basin was pretty cool. Had an inside and outside with
a grapevine lurching over the roof. The clientele couldn't be
more different than that of a Byron cafe. Byron was young.
Tourists were the big money deal for Byron. And they were

definitely young and from all over the world. Byron was a mecca for them.

And recently the call had gone out to the well-heeled young couples raising children and working from home in Sydney or Melbourne. 'Come to Byron and settle here.' And it worked. And a bloody lot of them had come Volvoing at speed up the coast. It was almost suburban now.

Here, down the coast, it was older. That didn't mean there wasn't a young crowd. But it wasn't sending out a call to 'come join'.

Leila at first was a little awkward with the place. Nothing big awkward but the pace was slower. No one was advertising themselves. That's what it was. That was the difference. Locals were pleasant but not going out of their way to win you. Which funnily was quite winning.

And they were funny, particularly the older blokes.

And they didn't try to chat her up, not like at Byron. Every bloke tried his luck in Byron, which Leila didn't mind. Leila knew how to look after herself.

Work for Leila would finish at three in the arvo, which she loved because it meant plenty of daylight still to be had.

There was a group class for yoga in the park on the way to the beach. The mums would plant their kids in the playground nearby and join class. There were a few Indigenous kids mucking around in the park or tearing down the hill on bikes. Not every day, but when they were there, they were having fun.

The camping ground was always full of travellers moving up and down the coast. Many were students taking a gap year or doing online studies and they swelled the yoga classes.

They sure did. Classes were Monday and Thursday.

There were vans aplenty by the beach and in the car park by the Point. There were sixties VW kombis in great condition and screaming with colour. Bedfords and old panel vans with kitchens and bunks. Young people were clever.

There was a house a couple of streets back from the beach that had been converted into four flats. Leila had the back one.

A wire screen door covered the front door. Its job was to keep the flies and mozzies out. Good luck with that. Inside was a bedroom, bathroom and decent size dining room and kitchen. Very clean and very near her work.

Leila was happy.

It took a week before Leila felt at home. Sometimes you never feel at home when you move. Just feel like an outsider.

Maybe it was because of working at The Basin. The Basin was a hub. Everyone passed through there at some time or other during the week. Some were there every morning for coffee and muffins. And they treated her great. Very warm, these Aussies. There were a couple of pains in the arse. Had to be but you worked out quickly how to treat them. A smile and quick service in most cases got them relaxed.

———

Leila began to learn names. First off, Benny, the most important name given that he was her boss.

Nolene was her favourite. She must have been in marketing, always with her tablet out and sending emails or making lists. Nolene wanted to know all about Leila from the first day they met. She had travelled widely and loved

Copenhagen. Last trip she stayed in a beautiful boutique hotel on the main street. Only sixty euros a night. Wonderful. Told Leila if she had any trouble with anyone to let her know and she'd sort them out.

Nolene's husband was Brian and he was always busy. It was Brian sorted out Leila's lease on the flat. Month to month with a month bond.

Wanda was a funny one, always scribbling in a notebook and making sure her dog had water. You could tell she had a few of the blokes dangling.

Sheila was always first in for a coffee each morning on her way to work. Pretty dry humour, Sheila. In fact that was sort of the Aussie way, it seemed. Leila was never quite sure when they were being serious. It wouldn't take long and she'd know them all.

———

Leila's flat had a small deck with the yard covered in trees and bushes. The bush the butterflies loved the most was a night-smelling jasmine. And didn't they love it. Backwards and forwards stealing the nectar. And weren't they magnificent and weren't they all different and weren't the colours delicious. Vivid.

Grey wings with green overlay.

Pure white.

And the best. A black butterfly with white lower wings and red and green spots running along the wings. And it was bigger than the others.

Butterfly.

Papillon.

A film Leila's mother made her watch during her conva-
lescence. Leila's mother loved the American actor Steve
McQueen and he starred in *Papillon*. He played Papillon.

The character had a butterfly tattooed on his body.

He was put in a terrible jail in French Guiana, always
trying to escape. A somewhat depressing film, Leila thought.

What a terrible nightmare jail must be. Locked in a room
with no control or freedom.

Poor Steve McQueen.

———

It was a full moon and Leila took herself for a wander down the
beach. As she neared the three-kilometre mark Leila realised a
surfer was out. On his own. Just him and his board and waves
and moon. Leila sat on the beach to watch. She didn't know
much about surfing but it was full-on at Byron and she had
gotten entranced by the beauty of surfing. How great it must
be to paddle out with the ocean splashing over you.

The surfer was good. She knew that. He caught wave
after wave. Riding them effortlessly. Guiding his board up
and down the wave's face. Moving forward to the front
of the board and then skipping back and turning the board
to the front of the wave then back skimming the face.

As Leila watched she couldn't help thinking of snowboarding back in Scandinavia. How she had loved tearing
down a slope in the same way this surfer was surely loving
his surf. And then the last snowboard holiday and Frederick
and the accident and the heartache and the pain. Physical
and mental.

Leila started to cry.

'I hope I haven't brought that on. Didn't know I was surfing that badly.'

Being caught up in her thoughts Leila hadn't noticed the surfer finish his wave and come out of the water.

'Oh no, on the contrary. It's such a beautiful night and you were so as one with the ocean I got a little overwhelmed. Forgive me.'

'Okay, I forgive you. Mind if I sit for a while? Too magical to head straight home.'

'Please, of course.'

And the surfer sat next to Leila and they looked out at the ocean and the runway of light the moon had made.

'You're the young lady at The Basin. Right?'

'Yep, that's me, Leila.'

'Ken. How you enjoying it? We're not being obnoxious bastards, I hope.'

'No, not at all. I'm enjoying it a great deal. Everyone is lovely.'

'That's good.'

'Do you often surf at night?'

'Sometimes on a full moon.'

'What about sharks?'

'Yep, they're there. Just got to hope they've had dinner.'

Leila laughed. This was the first proper conversation she'd had with a local. Cause she'd talked to others, but that was as the waitress.

'What do you do for work?'

'I'm a lawyer. Work at the Aboriginal Legal Service down at the next town.'

'Wow, that must be interesting.'

'Yep, I guess interesting could be the right word for it. I'm going back now if you fancy a lift?'

Leila wasn't sure if she wanted a lift, but she'd enjoyed talking with Ken and didn't want to be rude.

'Sure, thanks.'

They wandered to the spot behind the dunes where Ken's van was parked. There were a couple of cars and a second van parked in the lot. But Leila hadn't seen any other surfers out.

'What are these cars doing here?'

'Fishing further down the beach. Blokes love their fishing.'

While Ken strapped his board on, Leila's attention was taken by the van parked by the two other cars.

She could hear noise. Couldn't quite work out what it was.

And then she knew as she saw Wanda's head come up suddenly and just as suddenly disappear.

Different sort of fishing going on in there. Leila smiled. She was going to have to find out who was on the end of Wanda's line.

Ken dropped Leila home. He was a fair few years older but she did find him attractive. Oh fuck, not an older man. Got to get off that type of thinking. Not going there again.

Leila cooked up some dinner, poured a beer and carried it out onto the back deck. She stared up at the moon. Looked different from this side of the world or was she kidding herself?

18

Ryan was born in France, but he saw himself as an Iranian. His father, a Sunni Muslim who had fled Iran after the Cultural Revolution in 1979 because he was afraid of persecution, was not a doctor but a janitor in a hospital on the outskirts of Paris. His dreams of becoming a doctor were smashed by the Revolution as he found himself penniless in his new home. A marriage and three children meant every minute of his time needed to be devoted to earning money not studying.

Being a Muslim anywhere in the western world after the attack on the Twin Towers in New York on September the eleventh 2001 meant hate and loathing were part of your everyday living.

He and his family were spat on, yelled at and constantly made to fear for their lives.

But Ryan's father was a hero. He stood tall. At the hospital he was given the filthiest of jobs. He never complained.

'We must always rise above the shit, Ryan. We must see ourselves as beautiful no matter how others see us.'

Ryan worked hard at school. He also dealt in drugs. Many of the young men and women like him in the public housing estates were co-opted by the local dealers to help move their product.

Ryan never felt guilty. You can't afford to feel like that when you're poor. The desperate decisions taken by the people around him made simple moral judgements by others seem so much bullshit.

Ryan knew he was carrying death and passing it on to addicts but there was nothing else being offered them. No medical or emotional help. No home. No love. What Ryan passed on at least relieved the pain.

He knew there had to be more he could offer. His father had always talked with pride of the doctors in his family history. He knew his father felt a failure. That Ryan must not be a failure. Ryan would become a doctor. For himself and for his father.

———

It was during Ryan's last year of his second cycle at the Sorbonne that he began to pay attention to the organisation known as Médecins Sans Frontières. He was inspired to learn how a group of doctors in France in 1971 banded together to provide aid to people who were threatened by violence and armed conflict in countries far away from France. They were prepared to put their own lives at risk to save other lives that no one it seemed, gave a fuck about.

Fighting in Afghanistan had been going on forever. And now the Taliban were in control. It was an extremely dangerous place to be, but Médecins Sans Frontières had volunteers prepared to go over and administer aid to those Afghans needing help.

Ryan couldn't believe people could be so brave. That's what he needed to be, brave. Bravery was what he didn't show when he needed to, and it cost him. What price love.

Yep the past year hadn't been easy. He was finishing his sixth year. His concentration wavered. He got through but wasn't sure what sort of doctor he'd make. Who he wanted to look after. Even asked himself if he wanted to spend his life looking after people. He was wobbly. Maybe there was a place for him where he could be brave and help. He needed time to think. He needed to take a break.

University was free for Ryan as a French citizen. When he gained entrance to the Sorbonne, his father was proud. But when Ryan declared he was taking a year off he was worried for Ryan. He wanted Ryan to start a practice and heal people. That's what doctors were meant to do. They talked but he knew his son had earned the right to choose his own path, and so with his parents' blessing, Ryan could set out for Australia.

The plan was to be free of the worries of the world, to explore the world and to love the world.

Ryan knew that his generation was facing a world in great danger. The media never stopped telling them. It was rammed down their throats. But he also knew that life could be wonderful. His parents didn't go through the troubles they did for him to face doom.

'There will always be troubles, Ryan. That's what makes life wonderful. Because we will overcome them and enjoy the magic. You are our magic, Ryan.'

And so a trip to the other side of the world. A trip to a country so big most of Europe would be swallowed up in it, that was where he would go to find the magic.

And that's what had happened. He found Byron Bay and other young men and women like him seeking the magic.

Which was well and good, but Médecins Sans Frontières returned again and again to the inside of his brain, working its way around and then down into his soul and gotcha.

He googled and found they had an office in Sydney and so he would go to their office and he would help with office work for a few weeks. That was the plan.

He had made a great friendship with a young Danish woman, Leila, during his time in Byron Bay. They had swapped numbers and promised to stay in touch during their travels through Australia. And Leila was true to her word.

> Hi ryan r u loving medecins s f bet u r l am now further down the coast working at a coffee shop called the basin google it .. come stay people lovely very small beach town no Byron b
>
> Luv L xx

Ryan really looked forward to seeing Leila again soon.

19

He arrived at the bikie's property at 8 am. The gate of course had a NO ENTRY sign hanging off it. There was no lock but he was expected, so he pulled the gate open, drove through, and continued on along a gravel drive for some four hundred metres to a well-maintained old house. So many houses like it along the coast. Front bedroom with a veranda running from it, hiding a dining room and then continuing around the corner. There would be another couple of bedrooms sitting behind the front bedroom. Must have been built around the turn of the century, twentieth century. They knew how to build in the old days, that's for sure. Who the hell came up with the design back then and did he know there were a bloody lot of houses still hanging around thanks to him?

That's like a song a bloke listens to. May have been recorded fifty years before but the singer couldn't possibly realise that someone was eating their breakfast in the back of Timbuktu and listening to it now and enjoying it. Would have to bring a smile to the singer's face if they knew. Dead or alive.

He parked and wandered around to the back of the house. Another veranda. Called out. Nothing. Called out again. Nothing.

No four-wheel.

No bike.

No bikie.

Nothing.

He wasn't sure what to do. Where was this Ace bloke? He certainly wasn't going to have a snoop about so went back to his van to wait. An hour later he was still waiting. Fuck it, haven't got all day, got a bunker to build so started the van and drove off home. Wondered what that was all about. Fucker did say 'tomorrow' and today was 'tomorrow'.

———

It was a few days later at the co-op. A tap on the shoulder. The bikie.

'What happened to ya, GT?'

'I was there. I came out to the address you gave me. Long driveway to an old house. Called, but nothing.'

'Yeah, just fuckin' with ya. Sorry about that but I had an important business meeting suddenly. Got back to the house late and no way to get in touch. Tomorrow, okay?'

He really didn't want anything to do with this bloke. 'Important business meeting' meant drugs. What other businesses were the bikies into? Aged care facilities? He kinda liked that thought but didn't know where the fuck it came from. He could see bikies cleaning the arses of old folks and delivering them meals on their bikes. Bikes running up and down the corridors of the aged care homes.

'You hear me? Tomorrow, okay?'

'Yep, yep, tomorrow.'

'You can add on a half day for the time you wasted the other day. That should square things. See you tomorrow.'

———

The bunker was moving ahead steadily. He was packing his van with concrete pavers ordered through the co-op when the bikie had so rudely disturbed him. Bloody heavy things. There were sixty of them. Fact is the bikie wasn't rude at all and that was sort of scary. And not being at the property when they'd arranged. Was the fucking bikie playing with his head? Didn't need this. Stop, breathe. And he did. And he calmed down. Bloke just couldn't make it that's all and he's a nice guy, that's all.

The past couple of weeks had seen the excavation finish beneath the house. About a dozen posts with bearings, made sure the house stayed up. Planks now covered three walls. There were two air vents on one side wall leading out of the ground and attached to the shack's back wall about a metre up. Didn't want her to die from no fresh air.

He tapped into the junction box to get power. Electrical wires were sealed in four conduits threading down through the floor into the bunker, one behind each wall. Small lamps with unbreakable glass coverings were set into each wall and controlled from up in the house. Next was to build the ceiling and insulate it with soundproof batts. His guest needn't hear what was going on in the house.

Silence was the objective. That's how it was with the cubby house.

———

The next day he took another run out to the bikie's place. This time there were three bikes parked out the back of the house alongside Ace's four-wheel. And this time Ace was there, along with three pit bulls.

'Don't get out, GT. We're going for a little ride.'

About a half kilometre further along they came to a barn housing a tractor.

'You can get out now.'

He did. They stood staring at the barn.

'Need you to fix it.'

'What do you mean?'

'Look at it. You can see parts of it are fucked. Unfuck it.'

He walked around inside the barn. It was big but not huge. About the same length as the house, not as wide. All the gal on the roof was rusted through. It'd leak for sure in a decent rain. Some of the beams holding up the roof had seen better days. Better to replace them. There were three light fittings hanging from the beams. It was a wonder the place hadn't gone up in smoke ages ago. Deadset chance for an electrical fire. The floor was fine. A concrete slab had been laid a number of years ago but had stood the test of time. Obviously hadn't seen much wear.

The walls, also made of gal iron, needed work and the doors needed to be rebuilt.

'What d'you want to store in here?'

Ace looked at him.

'I'm getting you to fix the barn. What I'm doin' with it is no fuckin' concern to you.'

Bye bye Mr Nice Guy.

'Jokin' with ya, GT. Feed for the cows. Might get you to make a small stable for a horse or two in there later.'

He knew the bikie wouldn't have a clue which end of a horse was which and he wanted out. Out of the job. Out of the property.

'When can you start?'

'Well, I'm sort of up to my arse in work at the present. You might be better off finding someone more available.'

'Nope. I've settled on you. Let's go back to the house and work out a plan and budget.'

And they did.

And he didn't see the owners of the other two bikes.

And it had to be ready in no more than six weeks.

And he needed to get home and roll a big one.

———

Fella knew he could finish within the six weeks, but there was the bunker. That was a priority.

For most of that day he worked solidly preparing the ground for the pavers. His back screamed.

He didn't like being beholden to the bikie—or was it bikies now? Setting up some coin from the crop meant he could finish the barn and tell the bikies to find another handyman. He was over it.

At six he called it a day and decided it was time to pay Adrian a visit. Rang him and arranged to have coffee at The Basin the following day. He didn't sleep well that night.

There was so much going on in his head with the bikie shit. Must have taken a piss about a dozen times.

The next morning he was into the bunker at break of day. Work was good for him.

The pavers almost laid themselves, and then he had a couple of hours to work on the ceiling and the soundproofing.

———

Adrian was sitting outside at The Basin with another bloke when he pulled up. He parked the van and joined them.

Introductions and coffee orders followed.

'Benny runs The Basin. I've spoken to Benny about your crop. He's very interested. Was a gardener himself once, weren't you, Benny?'

'There was a time.'

There certainly was. When Benny first moved to the coast, most locals were gardeners. But drones and thieving kids made it all a little dangerous, so he became a business-man instead. Opened a coffee shop. The Basin.

'Nice crop.'

'Thanks. Did you try it?'

'Of course. I'm happy with the deal Adrian talked if you are. Pretty sure I can get rid of five bags. Gives us both a few extra bucks a week. Not too greedy. Greedy is the death.'

The coffees were delivered to the table. It was the blonde girl who delivered them.

Once she had left the table the conversation continued. The fella said he was happy with the deal. They finished their coffees and shook hands. It was decided delivery would be Tuesday nights at The Basin. First delivery after the weekend.

———

He didn't drive far. He parked the van closer to the beach but made sure he held The Basin in view. He turned on the radio. Figured he'd listen to one of those songs the singer had no idea he'd be listening to down here in Timbuktu. He smiled. Thinking is fun, he thought.

Just after three, the waitress left The Basin. She walked to the park, where she joined a bunch doing some exercise. Stretching and stuff. He couldn't help noticing she had a good figure. The exercise class took about an hour, and then she chatted for a while before walking back. She passed The Basin and turned into a street a bit along. He started the van and moved off, following her trail, turning into the same street. As he turned into the street he caught the back of her entering a yard and then she was gone.

It was obviously broken up into flats. He took note of the house number. All he needed to know now was which flat was hers.

20

He was pretty excited about the bunker. It was looking good. The last wall was in and he was now working on the stairway. He'd already fashioned the trapdoor out of old steel blades. Reinforced and cut them and welded them together. The guest room would be ready for a guest very soon. Exciting.

The bikie's barn was a big job. He could cut the timber he needed from his own property, but then having to cart it to their property would be difficult. He'd need a truck. He didn't have one, and nor did the bikies. He put it to Ace that he would cut the timber from the bikies' forest. He was fine with that. Then he could dress the planks there. Drag everything to the barn by tractor, much as he'd done at home with the bunker.

Once he'd prepared the barn, he was going to need help getting beams onto the roof. Bloody ropes and pulleys. He could handle replacing the gal by himself. Bit of a pain but doable. Easier with someone.

He was now two weeks in on the build. On his way home he stopped by the back door to the bikies' house. There were three bikes parked there and three big fucking scaries showing big snarly teeth. He definitely wasn't going to get out and knock on the door. Fuck no. End up with a shottie in his face. Why did he say yes to this job? What sort of fuckwit was he?

He hit the horn. Couple of blasts. Nothing. Waited. About to go again when the back door opened and out came Ace.

'Hey, mate, how's it goin'?'

Nice as pie.

'Yeah, good, but needed a word if you got time, otherwise it's okay, talk tomorrow.'

'Now's good. What's up?'

And he told him how he needed a hand cause the barn was more fucked than he thought.

And Ace told him how he didn't like that idea. Not at all.

He explained the need to the bikie. How he couldn't see any way round it really. Not if they wanted it finished in the time.

'Give me an extra few weeks, I might be able to do it myself.'

Ace thought for a bit. Told him to wait there, that he'd have to talk to the Don about it and went back into the house, closing the door after him.

The fella waited. The Don—what sort of shit was that?

The door finally opened and out came Ace with two other blokes. Obviously the owners of the other two bikes.

They stood looking at him in the van. He was shitting himself.

The three bikies chatted among themselves. It was obvious one of them had the say. Must have been the Don bloke. He was bigger than the other two. Wasn't sure if they were arguing but finally Ace came over.

'Okay, we don't like it. We all like our privacy, but if it has to be, then okay. You know who you gonna use?'

'Yeah, got a bloke in mind. Good bloke.'

'Right, then you bring him in and you go straight to the barn. No stopping here. Ever. Got it? And then straight out at the end of the day. Okay, me old mate?'

He told Ace that was all good. Told him he'd be back as soon as, and drove off. He knew the three bikies were watching him drive off.

He also knew this wouldn't be the only day he'd be shitting himself.

———

The next day he worked all morning on the stairway to the bunker, cleaned up and headed to The Basin.

Adrian could meet him at one-thirty. He parked the van once again opposite The Basin. The outside table was taken so he found a free one inside by the window. It was only one-twenty.

He liked this coffee shop. He also liked the blonde waitress who asked him what she could get him.

He ordered a coffee. He was glad he was early. It gave him time to watch the waitress.

He didn't stare. He was careful, just took her in. She was the one, he knew it.

Adrian arrived spot on one-thirty. He liked that.

Punctuality was very important. Adrian ordered a coffee. Another chance to watch her. She was classy. He liked class.

Adrian was keen to do a few weeks' work and was available whenever. Fella gave Adrian the lowdown. Bikies. Adrian laughed. It wasn't a problem. He knew the rules. See no evil, hear no evil.

It was arranged that he would pick up Adrian each day and then return him home. He didn't want Adrian coming to his place.

They drank up, paid and left The Basin. Adrian was off for an afternoon wave.

Fella waited in his van.

It wasn't long before the waitress finished work. He watched her leave. Would she go straight home or to the beach?

As she headed towards home, he started the van and wheeled off into her street, stopping past her house. He watched in his mirror as she walked around to a side door. Now he knew her flat.

21

There was a party going on at The Basin. A big party. Benny was throwing it for his great friend Conchita. It was her birthday. Told her to get her arse down to his place Saturday evening. And as Benny had told her, and as Benny had been a part of her life for most of her life, she did as she was told and took her arse down to The Basin for her party.

And boy didn't they go back.

———

Benny had lived across the road from Conchita when they were growing up in the Migrant Hostel in western Sydney. It was where a family waited to be given a house from the government. Wasn't just for migrants, though. Benny's father worked long hours on the wharves down at Sydney Harbour but was never able to make enough to buy a house, so the family lived in a Nissen hut. Nothing wrong with a Nissen hut while you waited for your own house.

Conchita had migrated to Australia as a kid and, like Benny, was at the hostel with her family waiting for a house. They played together, became friends.

As it happened, both families got houses in the same area in the southern suburbs of Sydney and so the friendship continued. In fact there were plenty of years when Conchita joined Benny's family on holidays. And now they each had their own coffee shop up the coast. Stranger things have happened, they thought, but not a lot.

Conchita got mixed up with an older bloke when she was only sixteen. Left school and moved in with him. Her family disowned her but Benny stayed in touch. When the relationship fell apart he was there for her, helped her get a job, and stayed her close friend.

Benny worked in hospitality, continually moving up the chain of command and eventually managing a coffee shop in the inner city. Then, when Benny had a choice of two cafes up the coast, he chose The Basin and helped Conchita into taking the other. He knew she'd know how to make it work.

———

Leila had been on duty most of the day setting up for the party. Benny had told her to go home for a couple of hours and get a rest before resuming work.

Leila hadn't been partying since Byron and she realised she'd missed it. Benny wanted to make it a great night for Conchita but he also wanted the staff to have fun. Memories of friends and dancing and laughing herself silly at Byron had Leila looking forward to the night. And she had heard from her very good friend Ryan that morning. A text in reply to hers.

> my dear friend leila ... miss you and will definitely be visiting you at the
> basin .. googled it. looks like another little paradise ... how beautiful
> are all these beaches, sydney full of them too and a harbour ... learning
> so much about medecins sans frontieres .. what an organisation. cant
> wait to tell you all about it ... keep in touch. ryan x

Ryan inspired Leila. Something about him made her smile. He was an optimist, that's what it was. She so looked forward to seeing him down the track.

————

There was a single bed and a couple of pillows. Sheets and an old sleeping bag. If she behaved he might buy her a blanket or two. Could get a little cold down there at night and the heat of the day might be a bit off. She could strip off, that would cool her down. He would give her a bucket with water and a potty just as Dave had given him. He struggled to get the bed down the stairway and into the bunker. It was from a second-hand shop on the highway. Got it for thirty dollars.

The bunker was finished. He ran his hands along the walls and smiled up at the ceiling.

Then he walked to the middle of the room, sat on the floor and cried. The cry became a howl. It came from deep within him. From some terrible place that had the control. It always had the control.

The bunker needed to be finished by today because today would be special like it was back then.

Back then when they had finally sealed the caravan in the backyard. All that showed was a trapdoor in the middle of the yard. Anyone asked they were told it was to do with the septic.

Dave was very pleased with himself. Went and got a bottle of beer to celebrate. Then got drunk. Then smacked him across the head. And then locked him in the caravan. That's where the howl came from.

Special day.

He made up the bed. Wanted everything to be tidy for her. Then he lay on it. If only she was here now. His mother. Dave hated her going down to him in the caravan. Comforting him like a baby. But when he was away at work, she would come down and lie with the fella, holding him until his crying eased.

Why wasn't she here now for him?

Finalising the stairway and sealing the last wall had been a lot of work. He'd worked well into the night and then first thing in the morning.

There was to be a party at The Basin tonight and there was no way he wouldn't be there. Not being invited wasn't a problem. He didn't need to be at the party so long as he could watch.

Early in the evening he closed up the bunker. He left a small lamp on, by the bed. He had a light installed in the stairwell. Didn't need to break his neck getting her down the stairs.

Back in the house he checked he had everything. The bottle and flannel, a towel and plastic ties, and of course a mask. Not that she'd be awake anyway. Still.

At six-thirty he drove to The Basin. He was excited. He parked the van in her street and then walked to the park opposite the cafe.

There was a park bench that gave him a decent view but kept him hidden. He looked for her but couldn't see her. Fuck. Looked some more. Left the bench for a tree with a better view. Scanned The Basin. Where was she?

She had to be there. It was a special night. Her special night.

22

Brian wasn't big on parties. Didn't mind small parties in the back of his van at night down behind the three-kilometre mark with Wanda. That was different. Loved that sort of party.

And now Nolene was on his back to get dressed because she was definitely in the mood for a party.

He really did love Nolene but he was getting very confused these days. Nolene had a bloody successful marketing business but it demanded she travel, leaving Brian alone and lonely. And so enter Wanda. And did Brian mean enter. Stop being dirty. What's with him, it was just a bit of a fling. Age. He had to admit nearing sixty had depressed him somewhat until he found a way out of the depression.

The problem with living in a beach town was you saw everyone nearly naked. In bathers, anyway. And if a woman had a good figure she wasn't going to hide it in a one-piece and Wanda's two-piece hid very little.

She had made good with a couple of the fellas, but those relationships didn't settle into anything lasting. Which was a bit like how it worked for everyone, mainly. No hard feelings and still friends. Wanda was a lot of fun but no drongo. Truth was she was smart. Wrote the odd piece for the local *Valley Courier*. Had a way with words. And her body. For fuck's sake, Brian was trying to get ready to go to a party and all he could think about was Wanda.

———

Nolene was an aspirational girl from way back. Might have to do with her mum being a trade union organiser and her dad being a teacher. She was always proud of her mum. Never took a backward step. It was from her mum, and her dad as well if it came to that, that she got her sense of justice, and didn't they know it around the beach. And didn't they respect her for it. It was because of that Brian fell hook line and sinker for her twenty years ago.

They were having dinner together at a Vietnamese restaurant. Brian had been set up with her by his best mate. Reckoned they'd get on like a house on fire. Nolene overheard a bloke at the next table refer to the Vietnamese waiter as a slant-eye. Nolene walked to the bloke's table, picked up a jug of water, poured it over the bloke's head and told him that he was a 'racist prick'. The restaurant broke out in enthusiastic applause. The bloke quickly paid and left the restaurant. Brian was in love with Nolene from that moment. Up front, was Nolene.

That's why he was so confused now.

———

Nolene had her party outfit on. Black top and pair of black jeans. Tapered. She looked smart. Brian had always liked the outfit. Told her many a time. He was a funny bloke, her Brian. She felt bad about leaving him on his own so often but the company had suddenly taken off and she knew you didn't look a gift horse in the mouth. 'Strike while the iron is hot' and 'make the most of it', all those bloody sayings, as old fashioned as they sounded, sounded truth to Nolene. And it was for their future she was going at it so hard. Yep, their future. She needed to hold on to that.

Brian had plenty to do, so she knew he wouldn't be sitting around. He was a worker her Brian, more than she could say for his father. Did bugger-all but drink. An alcoholic. Lasted no more than three months in any job. One after the other. Brian's mother had run off when he was fifteen. Ran as far as she could so she couldn't smell the bastard anymore. He wasn't abusive, none of that stuff. He was what they called a 'no-hoper'.

Brian tried to help his father but as the years went on his father deteriorated. Too many times Brian had to pick him up from some lane where the cops had found him senseless, covered in vomit or shit. Nolene respected how Brian rose above that curse and educated himself at agricultural college. Nolene reckoned it was cowboy movies that gave Brian a love of the land and there was plenty of land along the eastern seaboard of northern New South Wales necking into the many valleys running west of the Pacific Highway.

And he was funny. Funny dark at times, but still funny. Nolene reckoned Brian's sort of background either ground you down or you learnt to look back on it with irony. The irony that it didn't fuck you.

It was his humour that got her into the sack pretty well immediately on meeting him and then giggled her into marrying him. And they had a good marriage. Twenty years long. Only regret was no children. Nolene couldn't have any but that's life they both agreed. They had each other. A ten-hectare property nudged into a hill with forest all round and a river running through it gave them the calm they needed with their jobs. Brian had sold many a property like theirs to the city escapees who now longed to move to the coast. Real estate was his game and he was good at it.

She was going to give Brian plenty of attention tonight. He was definitely going to get lucky. She owed him. Party time at The Basin. Bring it on, she reckoned.

———

Wanda loved a party and always had for as far back as she could remember. And remembering far back took her to Greg, her first true love. Lust or love? Wanda knew the difference now, but when you're young they are entwined and come under the heading of romance: full-on, hot-as-hell, can't-think-straight, back-seat-of-a-car romance.

And that's where she was with Greg on the night she met him after a party, the back seat of his car, doing things that were mind-blowing. Greg loved her. Loved her most Saturday nights on that back seat of his old man's car.

And life and love moved on from there to now, doing almost the same thing with Brian in the back of his van. Except she knew the difference now. Definitely lust. Girl's got to get it where she can, even if it's on a blanket on the floor of Brian Slaviero's van with her head on a saddle. She knew Brian was married, but it takes two to tango so wasn't all her fault. Brian told her that she perked him up. Wanda was good at perking a bloke up who needed perking up.

A bunch of them had ended up laughing and drinking until late out front of The Basin after closing and takeaway Chinese. It had been a good night. A full moon night. Nolene had been out of town and Brian had been very funny.

When people started to head off, Brian offered Wanda a lift home. Nothing wrong with that. He was just being considerate. Of course it was Wanda who put her hand on Brian's thigh as they were driving. Couldn't remember why. Just put it there. Brian looked across at her. What is it with blokes? Next minute they were driving down the dirt road paralleling the beach to the three-kilometre parking spot. One kiss and then into the back. That's how it happened. Wanda put it down to nature. Got to blame something. Anyway, that was it. Once and once only. As if.

She did have to admit that he was a bit of alright, the old Brian. They'd said hello a couple of days ago, but Nolene, his wife, was with him and Wanda liked Nolene—everyone did—but she seemed to be out of town a fair bit lately.

Wanda checked herself in the mirror and quite liked what she saw. A vamp. Stop it, you naughty girl. Anyway, she was definitely going to have fun tonight. With someone. Maybe Nolene is out of town at the moment. Nope, not Brian, no way. She laughed.

'Plenty of surfers in the sea.'

Wanda opened the door of her house. Stepped out into the warm night air. She looked forward to the stroll to The Basin.

———

Sheila didn't really feel like a party given she had been cleaning all day. A bottle of vino and a dooby in front of the telly sounded fine to her. But after a few tokes of the dooby she started to think: why not? Not bad, the weed Benny had got hold of. A few of the locals were very impressed. Might be a good idea if Adrian had a few tokes. Might loosen him up a bit.

Yep, she was keen on the bastard, no doubt about that, but he was a hard one to figure out. It wasn't as though he was a bad arse, but there were times when he was completely impossible to communicate with.

Sheila wasn't even sure what Adrian did. She knew he helped out on construction with the chippies sometimes, but most of the time he seemed to be a free spirit. You'd see him about during the day, strolling or driving. Where to? Who knew?

Sheila wanted to know, that's who.

There hadn't been a bloke in Sheila's life for a few years. And that hadn't been a bloke, that had been a husband. A husband who ran off with a little surf bunny who came visiting the area. Two years ago exactly. At least he was good for one thing: her daughter. Her beautiful little Rosie.

Not little anymore. She was a big girl now in Melbourne studying at university. Rosie vet. Sheila loved the sound of that, but she missed Rosie being around. That's how it goes. You breed them, you feed them and you lose them, but you never stop loving them.

The good thing is Rosie does have a good relationship with her dad. Sheila wouldn't want it any other way. A dad is important. Sheila knows that only too well having lost her mum through cancer when Sheila was only twelve.

Her dad was fantastic. He was at every sporting carnival or prizegiving right through Sheila's school life. He was always there to help whenever, and there were a few whenevers.

Losing her mother did do something to Sheila's temperament, which led to sessions with doctors for a few years. But she came through all that. She fell in love, married and had Rosie. That was a blessed time, but things change. Sheila knew that and she was fine with it.

Sheila finished the dooby, went into the bathroom, dropped her working rags and let the hot water stream all over her. It felt good. Her body felt good. It was in good shape. Definitely in good enough shape to go a few rounds with Adrian.

Boy, she'd like to land Adrian.

So she'd better get a move on, get dressed and get to The Basin.

———

Adrian didn't smoke very often but he did have the occasional, so thought he might as well roll one now. That was the problem with the job. Made a bloke feel like a hypocrite at times but then that's how it works, can't be done any other way. So it was a light one he'd rolled, just a teaser.

He was going to the party. And why not, he needed a laugh. Hadn't had one in a while and knew he wouldn't be getting one over the next couple of weeks. Thought about the fella. He was a strange fella, no question, with his weed and now some connection to bikies. Adrian had noted the van's licence plate and had it checked out for an address but it was still registered down Newcastle way. A strange fella. 'Let's see where it goes' was always Adrian's motto and he intended to stay with it. It was dead set going somewhere interesting, he knew that.

Adrian could never work himself out. He knew he was capable, always had been right from the get-go. His old man was capable too. They reckoned he could handle anything, his old man. That's what got him killed, wasn't it? Send in the capable cop to talk the gunman down, get him to surrender. Fucker had held up a bank but the alarm had gone off and so he'd grabbed a customer as a hostage. And Adrian's father, the most capable cop, was sent in. And *boom*. Fucker didn't want to surrender so he shot Adrian's dad. Adrian was seventeen.

It hurt. They were close.

Adrian liked being up the coast. The city kept triggering memories for him. After his dad's death it was about keeping busy. Get the adrenaline flowing, that would make him forget. But it didn't. He lost his way for a bit. Nothing too bad. Used his brawn way too much over his brain. Met a whole lot of 'interesting' people and found out how the world really worked.

And then opportunity presented itself where his knowledge could be put to good use.

He took the opportunity and only a few years later found himself up the coast. Better.

And tonight he was going to a party. Needed to lighten up, he knew that. Maybe one of the ladies might fancy him and there were some fanciable ladies around, that was for sure.

He quite liked Sheila but he reckoned she'd run a mile seeing as she'd seen him being a grumpy bastard too often. Maybe Wanda or Conchita? He knew he was getting way in front of himself. Be lucky if he got a dance, let alone anything else. Maybe that's why Adrian put on clean jeans and a clean shirt. See what might happen at the party at The Basin.

———

Ken had enjoyed a tough week. An Aboriginal kid got himself rissoled, broke into a bottle shop and instead of knocking off a couple of bottles and pissing off, the stupid little bugger decided to drink the stolen booze in the shop, fell asleep and was found by the owner next morning passed out on the floor. The kid was charged with breaking, entering and stealing, and Ken was given the case to handle.

Ken had been working as a lawyer at the Aboriginal Legal Service for two and a half years, something he would never have imagined himself doing but knew had been a saver. He knew damn well it really did save him. Saved him from being a bitter, whingeing victim. Yep, Ken never stopped telling whoever wanted to listen just what a bloody dreadful time he'd had growing up.

He'd been a criminal lawyer for a few different firms for some ten years, dealing with the shit you deal with there, when he was asked to defend an Aboriginal woman accused of murder. Ken had never been in contact with an Indigenous person before. Truth was he'd never seen an Indigenous person except on the television.

But the case changed Ken. The woman had been part of the Stolen Generations. One of the stolen. Sent from welfare home to welfare home from the moment she was born. Abused and neglected, she'd had no chance in life. It made Ken realise that no matter how difficult his childhood had been there had been moments of happiness. There had also been a roof over his head and food and clothes and an education and . . . Yep, the case changed Ken.

The woman got ten years for manslaughter and killed herself inside in the first month of her incarceration.

Ken went looking to see how his ability as a lawyer could be better used. This led him to the Aboriginal Legal Service mob.

The past week he'd been backwards and forwards with the cops and the owner of the bottle shop. The kid had never been in strife with the cops before. Ken pushed the idea that as he'd done no heavy damage then maybe getting the kid to agree to attend the Macleay Vocational College was a better idea than hanging a criminal conviction on him. The college had been successful in turning around the lives of some fairly damaged kids. The kids didn't have to go to class, but that didn't mean they sat around playing on their phones. They could be out on the basketball court or in the library. They were to take responsibility for their own lives. And it was working.

The kid was all for it and full of remorse and willing to pay for the booze he'd drunk and any damage. He'd blown school dropping out early and was enthusiastic about getting back to learning, as he called it. The owner was a decent bloke but not entirely onside with the idea. Could the kid be trusted? Sergeant Gallagher supported the idea but made sure he scared the kid shitless first, with the thought of what it would be like inside. The sergeant told the owner that he knew the kid's family and they'd be on his back to behave. It was well worth a shot. A trying week for Ken, but a win. He would use tonight's party to celebrate the win. Might even get himself pissed.

———

Conchita loved Benny. Loved him like a brother, but given he wasn't her brother they never had fights. Much better way to have it. She loved the way Benny was resourceful. He always had been. You could see it in him as a young bloke. Nothing put him off. No seats left at the cinema didn't stop Benny hanging around until the last moment, and then the ticket seller would feel sorry for him and let him in.

He had a job at the local pharmacy after school when he was only twelve. Couple of days a week, helping unload the deliveries of medicines and pills and stack them on the shelves. Gave him pocket money because there wasn't extra dosh at home for pocket money. Bit of a goer, Benny.

It was thanks to Benny that Conchita had enjoyed camping up the coast. The two families were close but Conchita's family never left Sydney. They would make the most of holiday time at the beach or at the movies or just hanging. Then one holiday Benny asked Conchita's mum if Conchita could join his family camping. She loved it. Must have done it five or six times. Made Benny and Conchita close. Funny how it never led to a romance between the two of them.

The romance was with the wrong bloke. Dark times better forgotten. And at the end of that, there was Benny.

By then Benny was managing a coffee shop. He gave Conchita a job. Things looked up. And when Benny moved on to a bigger coffee shop, Conchita went along too.

It was during that time that Conchita had to be there for Benny. He fell madly in love with one of the waitresses. Head over heels. Benny was going to ask her to marry him. Told Conchita. But the waitress dumped him and ran off with one of the waiters. Broke Benny's heart. Softie.

This time Conchita helped Benny get through it. He came out the other end an even nicer bloke.

One evening he told Conchita he wanted her to join him up the coast. He had leased a coffee shop and there was another nearby that would be right for her. Conchita protested that she couldn't run a shop, but Benny said of course she could and he'd put down the bond. And he did and they both moved up the coast. Benny to The Basin and Conchita to Conchita's.

And now Benny was throwing a birthday party for her at The Basin. What a bloke. And it would be a lot of fun if Benny had anything to do with it. They were a good mob that hung out at The Basin. Something about surf culture. It's different. Hard to put a finger on it but surfers seemed to know something others didn't. Or was it that they were completely full of bullshit? Didn't matter. It would be a good night, that's for certain.

———

Benny looked in the mirror. Not bad, he thought. Not bad for a bloke with a bit of Leb blood in him. Benny's mother carried the Lebanese blood from her father. Her father had migrated to Australia in the late forties after the war. It didn't take him long to win over and marry an Aussie girl and bingo Benny's mum. So bloody lucky to not have straight-A Anglo skin just waiting for Mr Sun to come burn a hole through him.

The bloke in the mirror looked back at Benny.

'You the drug dealer?'

'You talkin' to me?'

Fuck, this was no joke. Benny turned away from the mirror. What had he got himself into? Bloody Adrian and the weed. Straighten up, you idiot, it's a few bags a week, nothing serious.

And then Benny got a bag out and started rolling a few. It was a party and a little weed would go down a treat.

It certainly helped with the shop rent, that was for sure. Rents were going through the roof up and down the coast. The regions were the place to be now. Should have been discovered years ago. And with the discovery that you can work from home with a computer in front of your face for eight hours and then go outside and dive into the Pacific blue then lo and behold, the coast was swarming.

Benny really wanted Conchita to have a good night. He looked after Conchita, didn't he? But why? Funny that, how some people are important to you. You wish them well in life. Benny wished Conchita well in life.

Thought it had something to do with her running off with the older bloke when she was still so young. Benny felt she'd had something stolen from her. Some years that she would never get back.

He remembered being over at Conchita's place one Sunday when Conchita and her older bloke came over to get the rest of her things. The bloke just stood by the car. Said nothing. Smoked. Conchita carried stuff from the house to the car by herself. Benny tried to help but she waved him away. Then they drove off and he didn't see her for ten years.

Yep, Conchita was going to have a bloody good party if Benny had anything to do with it.

And Benny had everything to do with it. He'd spent up big. Gone the whole hog. Champagne. A DJ. And Thai food cooked by one of the locals. She'd done it before and she was a great cook. So what could be better?

Benny continued to roll a few. That would make it better and it was good weed. Adrian had done right by him.

Adrian would be at the party. Not an easy bloke to get to know well. Benny thought sharing a spliff with Adrian might be the answer to that. So he rolled a big one.

———

Leila woke. Sat up. Where was she? In her flat, of course. She looked at her phone. It was six-thirty and Benny wanted her back at seven. She'd dropped off to sleep for an hour and a half and found herself with Frederick and Ryan and Benny and Conchita and her mother and father, whose wedding they were all attending. What is it with dreams? What are they telling us? Not a lot, Leila reckoned. Just a jumble of knowings crashing together looking to make sense. None of the dreams from the past hour made sense, she was sure of that.

Leila decided that she would use tonight to get a handle on all the locals and to find out who Wanda had been playing naughty with in the back of the van.

Ken would be there tonight she hoped. She had seen him a couple of times, to say hello to, since their conversation on the beach under the full moon but she was interested to know more about him. A full-moon surfer and lawyer who worked with Indigenous people. Definitely a story there. That's all, a story, not a romance. Been there, done that. Shame he's attractive, she thought.

And there was Benny and Conchita. What's with them? Leila thought it was great that Benny was so thoughtful. It wasn't as though they were together. Never any signs of togetherness but they were close. And he had really set out to make tonight a great night for Conchita. Good for him.

Leila was very happy, she realised. Sort of content in a new way. She was anonymous. Carrying nothing. A clean slate. Everyone says travelling makes you grow up. Gives you new knowledge with the new experiences.

Leila wondered what her next experience would be. Better not be fighting off a shark! She laughed and jumped in the shower. A hot shower and clean clothes was definitely the experience she needed before the party.

Then a text to her parents.

hi family. all good. big party tonight at work. really looking forward to it. Im going to save up and buy you tickets to come visit. might take a while. ha ha. you'd love it. love you and miss you xxx

If only they could see how capable she was. That she had moved on from her accident and broken heart. She wanted to look especially cool tonight. Didn't want to be the waitress. Wanted to be Leila. Checked herself in the mirror. Yep, cool.

Leila looked at her phone and the text. How amazing life had become for her generation. Her parents would now be reading her message. Just like that.

Leila left a lamp on inside the flat. She didn't know what shape she might be in after the party and didn't fancy tripping over something on her way to bed.

Then she closed the door and stepped out into the night and onto the street that led to The Basin.

There were a few cars parked by the side of the road, and a van. Leila couldn't help herself and had a peek into the back of the van. It was almost empty, just a few scattered tools. She was pretty sure it wasn't the Wanda van. Surfer blokes and their vans. Funny, aren't they, she thought, as she continued on to The Basin and the party.

23

He watched them arrive. All of them. He knew most of their faces. And then he saw her walking along the street. She had been at her flat when he parked. What if he'd bumped into her coming out of her yard onto the street? What would have happened then?

He went back to the bench and sat down. Leant back. Breaths. Big ones.

In. Out. In. Out.

He calmed down.

He would be okay. He was sure of that.

He was prepared.

It was time to enjoy the party.

———

And that's what happened for the next six hours. People enjoying themselves at Conchita's party.

He was fascinated. What was it with parties? How much can you laugh? How much can you shout? How much can you dance?

And then suddenly a speech and hugging and cheering and 'Happy Birthday'.

And then he was back there, at his birthday party. He was ten. She made him a cake with ten candles. Some of the kids from school were invited and brought him presents. He loved getting presents. One of the kids had made him a kite. Reckoned he'd spent a week working on it. It was really something. Great colours and flew like a bird. They all played with it in the backyard. Best present ever. And there was lemonade and Coca-Cola and ice cream. It was a great party. They must have played in the yard for hours.

The parents watched, sitting on chairs, drinking beer. There was a barbecue with sausages that Dave looked after, happily passing them around to the kids and their parents. A perfect family party, for him.

The bloke next door came in with his young son and daughter. She found him funny and laughed at his jokes. And then Dave called a stop to everything and asked for everyone's attention. It was time for 'Happy Birthday'. And everyone sang it. To him. Just him. He was the happiest he'd ever been. And he had his great present. The kite.

As day shifted to evening, the party wrapped up. People said their goodbyes and happy birthdays again to him.

He took his presents inside while she cleaned up. Dave sat inside drinking beer and watching the telly.

Right on dark she came inside, having finished in the yard, and sat beside the fella, looking at his presents.

'Laughed at Mister Next-Door's jokes there, eh? Fancy him, do you?' Dave asked.

She said nothing, but there was fear in her face.

'I think he's a dickhead. Suppose he pops in here during the day, eh, with the odd joke. Or with the odd something else on his mind, eh?'

Then he got up and walked over to her. Looked down at her. Grabbed her and lifted her up with one hand around her neck. He hit her hard, sending her stumbling to the floor. She fell onto the kite, smashing it.

'I'm going to the pub for a drink. It's been a big day. Need a bit of peace and quiet.'

And Dave turned and went out the door.

He picked up his great present. It was wrecked. She put her arms around him while he cried.

—

And now they were all singing 'Happy Birthday' to Conchita. And Benny, with his arm around Conchita, sang it loudest. At the end they took turns standing beside her for photos.

The fella watched.

Leila made sure the drinks flowed, carrying trays back and forth from behind the bar. Champagne, and plenty of it.

He watched her. Saw she tried a drink from every tray. One for them, one for her.

He watched her and smiled.

Benny wandered over to Adrian and offered him a toke on his rather large dooby.

Adrian took it. Puffed and gave it back.

'Nice weed, Adrian. Been easy to offload too. Thanks for sorting it out.'

'No problem.'

'The owner has just hiked the rent, so bit of extra dosh helps.'

'Glad to be of service, Benny.'

And then Adrian took a drink from Leila's tray and moved off. Benny watched him.

Good guy, bad guy, Benny wasn't sure.

Brian was covered in sweat. Nolene was being pretty raunchy, rubbing herself against him. No way she'd let him off the dance floor. John Travolta, eat your heart out, Brian reckoned.

And then he let it rip.

'GLOR-IA. GLORIA. GLOR-IA. GLORIA.'

And on and on with Van Morrison at the helm of THEM.

Nolene laughed. Her Brian was definitely going to get lucky tonight.

Adrian was leaning on the bar, taking in the party.

'Want to dance?' came from beside him.

Adrian turned to find Sheila standing there. Fuck, she looked good. Sexy. Adrian wondered if all cleaners were as sexy as Sheila.

'May as well.'

'Better be a bit more enthusiastic than that or you can dance with yourself.'

Adrian smiled. She was good.

'Love to.'

And he took Sheila's hand and led her onto the floor.

Benny rolled another dooby. He was now sitting with Wanda and Conchita and Ken.

The music was pounding. He lit up and offered the dooby to Conchita.

'No, thank you, darling. You know I don't partake.'

'I do.'

And Wanda took the dooby from Benny. Took a drag and passed it on to Ken, who passed it straight back to Benny.

'Don't smoke, Ken?'

'Not anymore. Too old.'

'You're not too old for me. Let's dance.' And Conchita shuffled Ken out to the other dancers.

'Guess it's just you and me will have to finish this little fella, then, Wanda.' And Benny passed the little fella to Wanda, who grinned.

Leila watched Conchita and Ken dancing. They looked great together. Much better than a young Leila and an older Ken. She had learnt her lesson. Still. Maybe next time.

Stop it, Leila.

———

He was leaning against the tree in the dark and watching like a hawk.

He thought about that. Watching like a hawk. Why not a kookaburra? More Australian. But a hawk really zoned in on its prey and that's what he was doing. Zoning in. There wasn't a move she made that he didn't follow. He was getting excited. He knew it wouldn't be long. It was past midnight but the party was still flying. It would end, he knew that, and then it was his turn to party.

He needed to sit and take breaths. In. Out. In. Out. Relax. And he did and he waited.

She could take all the time she liked. Didn't matter to him. He was prepared.

———

And then it did end. Just on two as they emptied out of The Basin and onto the street. In dribs and drabs. Shouts and yells and 'see yous later' floated up into the early morning night.

Brian led a fairly intoxicated Nolene to their van. He knew he was okay to drive. Five drinks in eight hours wouldn't move the needle anywhere near the limit. As he helped Nolene into her seat, Wanda shouted out 'goodnight' from the front of The Basin with a cheeky smile. Brazen, he thought, and tempting, as he threw back his 'goodnight'.

Leila caught Brian's 'goodnight' as it landed with Wanda and right away the bell sounded. Ding. Of course, Wanda and Brian. It had to be Brian's van. Naughty Brian. Naughty Wanda. Leila smiled. There was so much more she'd learn about the goings-on here on the coast. She couldn't wait.

Guests ambled across the road, filling cars or wandering off to nearby homes.

Adrian and Sheila wandered off into the night and into the park. They found a tree to slip behind as they embraced and passionately kissed.

He was watching.

He was watching Leila.

And Leila was now back at work, clearing up. Picking up glasses and emptying leftover plates of food into the bin.

He was annoyed at that. Leila cleaning up. She was a queen. Queens do not clean up everybody's shit.

Conchita and Benny and Ken stood talking. Most had left but a few were hanging about on the footpath in front of The Basin. Conchita hugged Benny and then took Ken's hand and they walked out onto the street.

They stood talking for a while. It was obvious some sort of decision was being made. And then Conchita dragged Ken into the park.

Benny was carrying boxes of empty champagne bottles to the lane at back of The Basin. All the bins were stationed there in their various colours denoting glass or paper or household rubbish.

They'd all be packed full for Monday's council pickup.

Leila was in the kitchen stacking and unstacking the dishwasher. The two of them had been at it for an hour and the place was starting to shape up.

Floors would need to be washed and tables cleaned, but Benny had organised a team to come in at five to deal with that.

Finally, Benny sat down at one of the tables. He called Leila over.

'You did a great job, Leila. Hope you had some fun.'

Leila joined him at the table.

'Yep, had a lot of fun. Lot of fun. Thanks, Benny.'

'You can lie in tomorrow. Sorry, today. Your day off. What you going to get up to?'

'Sleep, I reckon, and then the beach.'

Benny told Leila she could finish up and head home. Leila argued that she was happy to keep helping but Benny insisted.

Leila grabbed her backpack and gave him a kiss on the cheek.

''Night, Benny. It was a great party and Conchita was so happy. Lovely thing to do. I'll see you first thing Monday morning.'

And then Leila went out the front door of The Basin into the dark. She looked to the park opposite. No stragglers. In fact, no one at all. As it should be.

Leila smiled, thinking about her new life, and headed for home.

———

He had moved from the park to the corner of Leila's street. There were only two streetlights on her path home from The Basin and he was well hidden in a neighbouring garden. He watched her as she got nearer. It wouldn't be long now. And then Leila stopped, turned and walked back, heading towards the beach.

This wasn't the plan. Should he follow her? He had to. No choice. But to where? He couldn't be seen.

———

Leila loved the dark. She was used to it. So much dark in Copenhagen. Winter days were only seven hours of light. That's why all those television shows coming out of Scandinavia are set at night. No choice. What was the name of the political one? The one where the woman becomes prime minister. *Borgen*, that was it. Birgitte Nyborg, that was her name, the prime minister. Made Leila proud to be Danish. It must have attracted loads of tourists, just like

Crocodile Dundee had made everyone want to visit Down Under and put a shrimp on the barbie. So many people had seen *Borgen*. Scandi noir, they called it.

So different in Australia. That's what she noticed first. The blue Australian sky went from the ground on one side to the ground on the other side. And the ocean. How important the ocean was to the Australian people. That made Leila stop and turn back. She wanted to see and feel the ocean before bed.

———

He followed her, keeping to the shadows. At the beach she stripped down to her underwear and ran into the sea. She didn't swim out but rolled about in the shore break, jumping up and down, throwing her head back and laughing. He was hypnotised by Leila. He didn't know this joy. Why had he never known it?

And then Leila left the sea, picked up her clothes and backpack and began to run back home. He had to move fast, to get back before her. All his planning was unravelling. Deep breaths were needed. Not easy while you're running. He hid behind his van and waited as she came into the street.

Leila wasn't running now. She felt so good. The splash in the ocean had refreshed her.

She turned into her yard.

He left the cover of the van. Put on the mask. Followed silently. So silently. Back now with the plan.

Leila walked to her door. She searched for her key. It was somewhere in the backpack. She emptied the contents onto the grass and combed through them. Leila found her key and shoved everything back in the bag. Then she stopped still. She felt something. It made her uneasy. Leila's mother had told her when she was a little girl she had a sixth sense. Didn't help with Frederick.

She put the key in the lock and turned it.

As the door began to open and the lamp spilled light, Leila was grabbed from behind. A sweet-smelling cloth was placed over her mouth and nose. She struggled and then collapsed.

He held her, keeping her from dropping to the ground. Mustn't wake the other flats. Then he moved inside, closed the door and carried Leila to the lounge.

———

Morning light hadn't arrived when the 5 am cleaning crew woke Benny. He'd passed out on the sofa. It was the only sofa. Otherwise tables and chairs.

The Basin opened at six-thirty. When the staff arrived he'd help set up then have the morning off for a sleep. Benny was pleased with the party for Conchita. Reckoned she'd enjoyed herself and might even still be enjoying herself with Ken. Benny smiled at the thought.

———

Back in the house he packed her bag and backpack. Then went through the flat one more time to make sure nothing was left. He placed the envelope on the table and walked to the door, placing the key in the lock. Now to get her to her new home. The bunker. He carried Leila to the van. Had to be quick—who knew when the first joggers or surfers would pass by and he didn't plan on being caught carrying a body.

He sat in the driver's seat, not moving. He had done it. He removed his mask. Closed his eyes and took his breaths. In. Out. In. Out. For three minutes. He opened his eyes and looked behind him in the van.

Leila lay there at peace. She'd be out for a couple of hours. Bloke he got the drugs from guaranteed it.

'Won't kill her but she'll be all yours for a while, mate. That'll be five hundred bucks.'

Time to get going.

The van moved off, driving past The Basin. It had been a very good party indeed.

———

Benny came out onto the footpath for some air and caught sight of the arse-end of a van charging up the hill. He wondered whose it was. Hoped it wasn't a partygoer. Well, not one over the limit.

The cops would have known about the party. They didn't muck around, the cops on the coast. Speeding and drink driving were about the only crimes they had to attend to up here.

Slow place, the coast.

24

Anna's passport finally arrived. Felt like forever. It was happening. Really happening. Anna rang and told José. Asked if he'd had any luck with the loan. And he had. It was all sorted. He would see her in São Paulo and take her to the plane for her trip to Australia. This was it. Did she want this? It was not even a question. She was going to Australia. To wonderland. José said he'd be in touch with details. Be about three weeks.

Three weeks. Anna couldn't keep her excitement in. Hardly slept that night. When she did, she was fruit picking. And dancing. And laughing by the ocean.

Anna's long-time best friend was Francesca. They had gone through school together forever. From nearly babies. Francesca was a beauty. Real beauty not pretty like Anna, but proper real beautiful. They would go dancing together at bars and clubs in São Carlos. They knew everyone. All the boys would watch and cheer.

And then he arrived. Rod with his long, dark, wavy hair. And Rod swept Francesca off her feet and into his arms.

Anna and Francesca didn't dance together anymore. Rod and Francesca danced together.

Anna was happy for her friend, who had found love with Rod. But it meant that Anna saw a lot less of Francesca. That drifted into some weeks of not seeing each other, and then months.

When Anna did next see Francesca, she was shocked. Her beautiful friend was almost unrecognisable. She had lost so much weight. She looked sickly. She was a junkie. She begged Anna for help. Anna took Francesca home. Made room for her in her bed. But Anna had to work, and even though Francesca promised to stay clean, Anna knew the struggle each day that Francesca must deal with.

Deal with. Rod was a dealer. Drug dealer. It was because of that *filho da puta* that Anna's best friend was in the hands of the devil. And the devil led Rod again to Francesca. And that was it. No going forward, only back. Rod took away Francesca's light. Dimmed it and then turned it off.

At Francesca's funeral Anna vowed she would not end up like her friend. In the devil's grip.

Three weeks and Anna would fly away.

25

He reckoned the drive home was the best drive he'd ever had. Was like floating not driving. Couldn't feel the road. And the sun was coming up and the morning light was like out of one of those paintings in art galleries. Not that he'd been to many. Really only been to one. The one in Sydney up from Circular Quay through the botanic garden. It was right before his mum died. She'd always wanted a ride on a Sydney ferry and a trip to the Art Gallery. And he was up for it. Up for doing special things with his mum since the evil bastard had gone. He loved seeing her happy. Shame that didn't last longer. Being happy. She deserved it after what she'd put up with. So one day they drove the Monaro down to Manly and caught a ferry and visited the Art Gallery. And that's where he saw the painting with the morning light. It was a bunch of blokes. Soldiers on horseback with guns charging across the land. It was so great. Whoever painted it was a genius. Every face of the soldiers and the faces of the horses was super charged with excitement going into battle.

Brilliant. That's what she said about the painter. He was brilliant. He didn't know how someone had the ability to paint like that. So fucking real. The light stayed with him. He'd see it sometimes. In his head. Thought about those soldiers charging into battle. Like him now charging home with Leila in the back of the van.

The gates had been left open. He drove straight through and parked behind the shed. Then walked back and chained the gates closed.

He was so high he couldn't believe it. Nearly bursting. Phew. He stopped. Leant against the shed. Steadied himself. Closed his eyes. Counted to ten. Slowly. Better. Thought it through.

He went to the trapdoor and lifted it. The two doors at the bottom of the stairs leading into the bunker were open. He couldn't remember doing that earlier. Too excited. The light was on in the room. It was time.

He went back to the van. Leila was still. He carefully lifted and then carried her across the yard and down the steps into the bunker.

He laid her on the small bed. It would be a little while before she came to. And when she came to she would be hungry and thirsty. He went up to his shack and found biscuits and water that he placed on a small table beside her. He pulled a light blanket over Leila and then sat on the side of the bed watching her. Eventually he stood up. It was time to leave.

There was work to be done.

———

Adrian struggled. Shouldn't have told the fucker he'd work the day after the party, but he needed to show his enthusiasm. Wouldn't go down well if he was replaced. Sweat poured off him. He'd been having fun, that's why he ended up like this. Too many doobies and too much grog. Hadn't done that for a while. And of course mucking around with Sheila was fun and an excuse to keep indulging. Must have pissed her off though, not taking her home. It was fun grappling in the park. They nearly had it off there. Sheila was certainly game for it, but somehow sense got into his thick skull and he excused himself from the clutching and made it home. He reckoned Sheila must wonder what the fuck was wrong with him. He also hoped he'd get another shot. Probably not. She wasn't stupid. But then again she might be desperate. Who knows? What he did know was the logs were heavy, extra heavy with his head feeling the way it did.

Fella was a strange one, that's for sure. Made sure he picked Adrian up. Obviously didn't want Adrian coming to his house. Adrian knew about the weed, so what was there to hide? Adrian would find out later, but for now it was the bikies that interested him. Everyone knew about the bikies. Drugs and bikies. They go together. And now he and the fella were fixing up a barn for bikies. Gotta be something interesting in that.

———

The fella knew Adrian was feeling it. Had to be feeling it given the good times only a few hours before. And he knew because he was behind the tree hiding. And he clocked Adrian singing and dancing and doobying with the ladies and then trying to fuck one of them in the park. Didn't happen though. Lucky. Doubt he'd have made it to work if he did. And then where would he get another worker? And then it would have been his fault because he supplied the weed. Boy, life's complicated.

He was having trouble concentrating. Couldn't stop thinking about her in the bunker. She was his.

She'd be awake now, he reckoned. She'd be wondering where she was. How she got there.

He was so fucking happy with himself. He planned it and he pulled it off. He was smart, not stupid like Dave always said he was.

But now it was fix this barn for the bikies and that meant hard work for at least the next month. Knew they had something on. Must be to do with drugs. Better not to think about it. Didn't fancy a bullet in the head. He would just get this barn finished, get his dough and leave the bikies to whatever. None of his business.

———

End of the day they packed up the van. Closed the barn. Tidied up and motored out.

But of course, of fucking course, Ace stopped them on the way out. Shit, he didn't want this. Less he had to do with him the better. And they were all there at the house. All three bikes were parked looking out like the fucking huge pit bulls, waiting for you to make a mistake.

He wound down the window. Ace shoved his big head in. Looked at Adrian.

'Thought I best say hello to your mate here.'

'Oh yeah, this is Adrian.'

'Great you could help, mate, appreciate it. Call me Ace.'

'Not a prob, Ace. Could do with a bit of extra dosh.'

'Good. Reminds me. Thought I'd pay you blokes a week upfront. Know you ain't gonna skip. And it's only gonna burn a hole in my pocket.'

Ace handed the fella a bundle of cash.

'Four grand there. Big day on the TAB. Four hundred a day each for five days. You can tell me at the end what I owe you for materials and machinery.'

Fella counted out the dough he'd been given.

'Great, that's great. We'll see you tomorrow around eight. Ta.'

'Yep. I know I'll be seeing you, you've got my dough. Oh yeah, by the way, GT, gonna need a couple of toilets put in.'

Ace laughed, pulled his head out of the window and stepped aside. Fella kicked the van over and drove off.

———

'Fuckin' toilets. Shit, no wonder he paid in advance. Never mentioned that before. This is getting bigger than Ben Hur. Whatever Ben Hur is.'

The fella passed over a bundle of notes to Adrian.

'Here's your two G's. Why'd I say yes to a bikie?'

Adrian looked at the notes in his hand. Began to count them.

'See no evil, hear no evil.'

On the drive home Adrian took out his phone. Tapped something into it.

26

Conchita had woken with a man beside her for the first time in God knows how long. There had been a couple of times but her teen years with the older bloke had really fucked her up. She had no idea what a relationship was after that time with him. It had been ten years. From sixteen to twenty-six. Formative years, a psychologist said. Whatever that meant. Aren't you always being formed? One year after the other. She'd thought it was love. Love forever. But it also meant no connection with family, doing things his way and not working while he did. Every day. It meant she didn't finish school, and so was useless for any decent job when she went hunting after it was over with him. After he'd kicked her out and moved on with a new, younger version.

She'd stayed clear of romance after him. Didn't trust it. Didn't know what was going to be asked of her. More control?

The psychologist said it was emotional abuse she'd suffered. He'd never hit her. Never. But he made her cry.

Made her think every time they argued it was her fault. Lost all confidence. Try going out into the world like that. And that's why she adored Benny. He'd helped her back to some sanity. And now twenty years on she has a cafe named after her and a man by her side in bed. Scary and exciting. Sort of terrifying, really.

She had always noticed Ken. He was a bloody lawyer. What would he see in her? Always liked him but never thought anything could happen between them. Not like this. Sweet Jesus. Scary.

It had started innocently enough. A dance. A drink. A chat. More dancing. Laughter. A cuddle. Fun. Just fun, like she hadn't had since forever. Like she had steered away from.

And now he was beside her in bed. And she had enjoyed it. The intimacy. He was considerate in making her happy. She hoped she made him happy.

There had been a lot of awkwardness in getting to this point, that was for sure. They'd walked off from the party hand in hand across to the park. They both lived in the same direction. So who was going to make the suggestion as to whose place they'd go to.

She certainly wasn't going to suggest it. And then they found a tree to lean against and the kissing started and got heavy and then Conchita suggested it.

'Want to come back to my place?'

And now there was a man in her bed. And Conchita was very happy about it as she snuggled up to Ken. She was bloody going to enjoy this. Just let go and stop being scared. 'It is what it is.' Another thing the psychologist said. He had a few sayings like that. Pretty good sayings, Conchita thought.

Ken turned to her.

'What would you like to do today?'

Conchita nearly burst. He wasn't racing off. They were going to spend the day together. He deserved something special. And Conchita was definitely going to provide it.

———

Nolene was still buzzing from the party. She'd had such a fucking good time, she told Brian as she handed him a coffee while he lay spent under the covers. Spent, as in hungover and sexually gratified. Brian liked being sexually gratified.

'Are you sexually gratified?' Nolene had asked him.

Classier than: 'Have you been fucked senseless?'

Nolene hadn't mucked around. In the van on the way home she'd mentioned something about 'particular desires'. And as soon as they got home she'd steered him to the bedroom and into the bed and into her. Nolene never did anything in half measures, which was why Brian was now sexually gratified. Maybe Nolene had started watching porn. If so, it was fine by Brian.

Of course, Nolene didn't know that Brian was comparing his 'roll in the van' with Wanda to his recently completed root with Nolene. Nolene was looking good, but the illicit nature of a night with Wanda was pretty competitive, he believed.

Brian couldn't believe he was thinking like this. There were not going to be any more 'rolls in the van' with Wanda. No way. A slip-up. Played to his ego. He was better than that. And then Nolene mentioned that she needed to be in Melbourne for an important business meeting later in the month. And Brian's mind went into overdrive with all sorts of thoughts. Predominantly regarding sex with Wanda.

Brian was beginning to wonder who he was.

———

Nolene slid back into bed with her Brian. Cuddled up to him. Shared his coffee. She had really enjoyed the night. She missed seeing the locals, what with travelling for business and then working from home most of the time. Last night reminded her of how much she enjoyed the locals. They were a fun crowd. She was also reminded of how everyone has a story, like she had and Brian had. Not better or worse, just their own story and struggle.

Nolene was quite sure what her struggle was at the moment. It would pass. Always did.

———

Benny snatched a couple of hours' sleep and was back on deck by nine. Didn't feel crash hot but knew the party had been a success and Conchita had enjoyed herself. That's all that mattered. Maybe 'enjoyed' was a little understated. That's what Benny hoped. He'd seen her wander off with Ken.

Benny had never known of any romance for Conchita since back when. He could only hope.

Romance. Not out there for Benny either. Not since that waiter left him in the lurch. Told Conchita and the family he'd been given the elbow by one of the waitresses, but that wasn't the case. It was a bloke. He couldn't tell anyone about him. He had great parents but an uncle on the Lebanese side had been disowned by the family for being gay and Benny didn't want that. He kept his secret to himself. He wasn't lonely. He had his business. That kept him busy. The Basin was full-on. If a bloke wasn't careful he could go under. Didn't matter how well you were going, you were always on a precipice when you owned a small business.

Yep, that stopped him being lonely. And there were friends. Conchita and his customers. Like a family. But sometimes Benny thought a companion might be nice.

———

The water was just what she needed. She dived deep, pulling herself along the sandy bottom. It felt so good. So good. Cleared the head. As Wanda came to the surface she could feel her body saying 'thank you'. She had gone in at the Point and swum to the beach. One arm after the other. Taking a breath after two strokes. She felt like a little girl again, swimming at the Brighton Baths from pylon to pylon. That was where she got her bronze medallion. That's right, she had a bronze. Didn't need some deadshit like Brian or any other male.

Back on the beach, Wanda dried off and lay down on her towel. The sun was good, working its way through her body. Invigorating. She thought about last night. It was pretty good fun. Maybe a dooby and a champagne too many, but hey, a girl has to live. She liked Brian. Even if he was a dill. He made her laugh. There would be other times, Wanda was sure of that. Hopefully he would be at The Basin later. She hoped so. What about the sisterhood? Screw the sisterhood when a girl gets randy.

She needed a distraction. She needed to get back to what she was good at. She needed to write another piece for the *Courier*, and not a lifestyle piece. Something with some balls. Which made her think of Brian. And with that thought Wanda raced in for another swim.

———

There was a house to clean, short-term lease with guests coming in that afternoon. Helped her save some extra coin, but short-term rentals were a problem all along the coast. People buying houses as investments and leasing them out for two nights or a week. Never much more than two weeks. Make more money if a couple of days at a time. Influenced rents for those who had been living in the area for a while. Influenced rents up and up. Some tenants were being forced out. It stank but that's capitalism. Chasing the buck.

Sheila was glad that she and Adrian went their separate ways after their grope in the park.

What bullshit. She was so up for it. Bloody Adrian. Bloody moody Adrian. So close. Reckon she had him. And then he begged off, saying he had early morning work on. Maybe he did, but even a quick root was okay with Sheila. That'd make him come back for more. But wasn't meant to be. Still, she'd got closer than any time before. There will be another time, you watch. Meanwhile, mop the bathroom. She laughed. Life's okay.

———

As the morning turned into afternoon, they dragged themselves into The Basin. Nolene and Brian and Ken and

Conchita. Wanda arrived around midday and Sheila not long after. Adrian was a no-go. They all confirmed it was a great party.

Benny made sure there were coffees all round.

'On the house.'

And in unison: 'Thanks, Benny.'

Wanda watched Nolene put her arm around Brian and snuggle into his neck.

'Good night, Brian?'

All heads turned to Brian but it was Nolene who answered Wanda.

'Oh yeah, Brian had a great night. Didn't you, darling?'

And then laughter all round at Brian's embarrassment.

Wanda smiled. If Brian wanted any further naughty with her then he was going to have to come crawling, that was for sure.

Benny brought out food.

'Leftovers.'

It would be a lazy afternoon.

———

Ken left The Basin to get his board as the sun was sliding towards the horizon. A southerly swell was pushing up long walls. It was going to be nice. A couple of hours of cruising before dark.

He walked through the park to the Point. The park still had people finishing off late lunches. A family was setting up a barbie. He walked over.

'Hi, Wayne.'

Wayne turned and beamed at Ken, grabbing him in an almighty hug.

'Hey, Gran, this the lawyer bloke sorted out the bottle shop stuff and the college stuff.'

Wayne stepped back and pointed to an elderly lady.

'This my gran, Moira, my sister Marcia, and this fella here, my little brother David.'

Moira put out her hand to Ken. He took it.

'Really grateful for what you did in helping Wayne. You looked after my boy really good. He's a good boy but sometimes the idiot pops out. He's meant to be showing his brother the right way in life.'

David put his hand out to shake Ken's.

'You won't be needing to look after me. I ain't gonna ever need no lawyer. You don't need worry about me, Gran, I know the right way.'

Ken shook David's hand.

'Sounds good. Reckon your brother's learnt his lesson now?'

Wayne put his arm over his little brother's shoulder.

'Yep, learnt it good. No shit from me anymore. You going for a surf, bro?'

'Sure am. Enjoy the evening.'

Ken hoped Wayne would honour the agreement made with the cops and the bottle shop owner.

———

As Ken hit the surf, the van drove past on its way to dropping Adrian home. Pulled up in front of Adrian's.

'Pick you up at seven in the morning, mate.'

'I'll be ready. Thanks for today.'

Inside, Adrian grabbed a beer from the fridge and took a

swig. He placed the bottle on the floor beside his chair and took out his phone. He found the message he'd tapped into it. Dialled. Waited.

'Hi.'

And he leant back in his chair as he read out the regos of the three bikes.

27

Fella parked the van beside the shed. Stepped out and opened the shed door. Looked at the Monaro. Opened the Monaro door and sat behind the wheel. He put his hands on the wheel and closed his eyes. He saw his father driving the Monaro with his mother alongside. He saw himself in the back. He let his mind scroll through moments they'd had as a family on outings. Scrolled only the good moments. This was a time only for the good. He smiled. Then he got out and walked across to the trapdoor.

He lifted the trapdoor and walked down the stairs. Stood behind the door. He opened the first door. Saw her through the bars. She was lying on the bed facing away from the door. Was she asleep? Couldn't tell.

And then she turned. Saw him.

She was absolutely the right one. He knew that. She was his now, in his bunker.

Leila screamed at him, jumped off the bed. 'What the fuck is this? What the fuck are you doing? Where the fuck am I?' And then she dropped to her knees sobbing.

He watched her. He was happy. He shut the wooden door and walked back up the stairs. He closed the trapdoor and walked into the shack.

The inside of the shack was coming together. He'd been able to put some work in on it. Mainly in the evening. He had the time. That's one thing he did have. It wasn't as though he had friends. Adrian couldn't be called a friend. Not yet. Adrian worked for him—that didn't make him a friend. They were in business together with the weed, but that only made them business partners, not friends.

She would be his friend.

———

They sat around a table drinking beer. It had been a long day. Began with an early morning meeting over the phone with Sydney and Melbourne. The Don did all the talking. Talking about pickup locations, schedules and final numbers.

The meeting ended up going fine. All was still in place. The delivery was somewhere between four and six weeks away. The cargo was fresh and ready to go. There would be another call in two weeks.

The rest of the day involved running around to the agreed drop-offs. And there were plenty of drop-offs, covering some two hundred kilometres of coastline. Sort of fun. Business fun.

End of the day, the Don made a call to Rio, to their man on the ground, José. José knew his way around. They had worked together a number of times. He had overseen at least ten deliveries in the past three years. All profitable and all went without a hitch. The Don had flown to Brazil five years earlier to suss out how bringing in gear from South America might work. He knew it would work, that was a given. It was the how that meant everything, and that's where the Don shone.

He wasn't the Don then. He was just plain old Don. Donny, they called him, and he hated it. And then one night on the telly they were showing this old movie called *The Godfather*. Donny loved it. Marlon Brando. What a legend. Don Corleone, mafia boss. The king. That night Donny became 'the Don'.

It was José who suggested the new cargo. A deadset goer, he reckoned. South American cargo. Delicious. All would be good even though it was new. For them. Others had done it with Thailand and the Philippines. So why not South America, José suggested. Brazil, Argentina, Venezuela. Gonna be a shitload of money in it and not just a one-off payday. Plenty of paydays. José was on top of it.

It had taken a bit of work persuading some locations that they were now doing business with the bikies. The Don had some experience in persuasion, so not a problem. Maybe a couple of problems, but 'fear eats the soul', so they say. Whatever that meant but sounded good.

And now they were sitting around the table.

'We get first taste?' Ace wanted to know.

'Of course, Ace. Same as always.'

'Fear eats the soul.'

And they laughed.

'To South America.'

'Definitely going to need those two toilets,' the Don laughed.

———

Leila sat on the floor of the bunker. She had eventually stopped crying. She stared through the grille to the door. Solid wood. Wasn't going to get through that. Leila knew that this wasn't good. You read about this sort of horror in books or films or the television. This sort of stuff didn't happen in real life. But Leila knew now it did. And it was happening to her. She knew him. She'd served him at The Basin. Her mind was in freefall.

Leila stood up. Was he watching her? Where was the camera?

Leila searched the walls, the roof. Nothing. If there was a camera it was well hidden. Leila sat back on the bed. There was food by the bed. She was hungry. She ate it and drank the water that was there. If she was to get out of this she would need her strength and her intelligence.

And then the light went out.

28

David loved his Pedal Ranger 3. It gave him a freedom. A freedom to roam. Now he could really discover his land. The land of the Gumbaynggirr people. It was so great what he was learning now. About his people. Moira told him stories about way back when she was a girl. When she was stolen from her mother. David had thought about that a lot. He couldn't understand it. How do you get stolen from your parents? Sure, he didn't live with his mum, but that was different. She got sick after David's dad was killed, and got herself into trouble with grog and stuff because she missed him. But Moira was there for them. Him and Marcia and Wayne. And they were there for each other. Not strangers looking after them. His case was different, very different.

David knew you could get into trouble if you didn't have someone who loved you to look after you. Like Wayne had got into some strife with the bottle shop, but that got sorted by the lawyer bloke Ken from the Legal Service, and Moira read him the riot act. But they were a family and families look after each other. No way David was going to get into any strife.

And now he was on his Pedal Ranger 3 and going everywhere. So many fire trails through the forests. And the Pedal Ranger 3 was a mountain bike and it could handle fire trails and dirt tracks easy as.

Some dirt tracks are more than tracks. They are wide enough for a truck or four-wheel and lead to driveways. Farms with big acreage or small acreage or in-between acreage. You never know when you take them if you'll end up on top of a mountain looking out over a valley or down into a valley with locked gates stating KEEP OUT. And now David was in front of a KEEP OUT.

David was a stickybeak. Couldn't help himself. Why would a person have KEEP OUT on their gate? For weed, of course. David wasn't stupid. But there was no one around. Might as well have a peek. What would they do, shoot him? He'd watched the joint for twenty minutes and hadn't seen anyone. Quiet as. Climb under the barbed wire. Quietly sneak past the gummies and bush and then David is by a shed. What's in the shed? Bags and bags of weed? Better take a look. Fuck me dead, it can't be. It's a deadset classic. An orange HQ GTS Monaro with a black stripe down the bonnet. David had a poster of that exact beast on the wall in his bedroom. Mind-blowing. And David decided then and there he didn't want his mind blown so he'd better hop it before he got spotted.

So David hopped it. Cycled home and went straight to his room. Yep, an orange HQ GTS Monaro with a black

stripe down the bonnet, there on a poster above his bed.
Wait until he tells his mates.

———

It was nearly a week since the party. Wanda had an idea
for a piece for the *Courier*. She was definitely getting
back into journalist mode and thinking of topics. Coastal
topics. And of course tourists sprang to mind. Not money-
spending tourists but backpackers. The bright, intelligent
young men and women from across the globe. The whys
and hows of being in Australia. There were thousands
of them not just touring the coast but crisscrossing the
country and working their arses off picking fruit and other
backbreaking jobs the Aussie kids were too lazy or spoilt to
take on. Wanda couldn't work that out. She was probably
being a little harsh on the Aussie kids, but back in her day
everyone wanted a stint in the country. Good fun. Might
even get laid. For sure. Wanda chuckled to herself at her
thoughts.

The Basin was where the young Danish girl worked and
she was a bright young thing, so Wanda made that her first
port of call. Not a good call though. Benny told her that Leila
hadn't fronted for work since the party. He'd tried to ring
her on the Monday but no-go. Then he went around to her
house, but again no-go. He was pissed off and surprised.
She was a good worker and punctual. Didn't turn up for
her next two shifts either. Benny asked Brian what he knew,
given he'd sorted out her flat. Brian went round and found
the flat empty except for an envelope with fifty dollars in it.
Written on the envelope was 'thanks'. Brian guessed the fifty

dollars was for cleaning. If you were lucky. Might get the kitchen cleaned for fifty.

They both thought it strange. Leila didn't seem like a flake, but who knows maybe she'd had a better offer from who knows who and decided to clear out.

Wanda was disappointed. She really needed to up her game and get back to writing. But not the usual syrupy tripe that the local rags put out. Wanda was better than that. She was going to need a rethink.

———

It hadn't been easy getting a gig with Médecins Sans Frontières. Even though it was the Sydney office and probably a little more laidback than their European offices, they were still security conscious. There were over sixty-eight thousand staff working in some pretty hostile environments. The hostility could spill over. Staff on return needed to be looked after. They had seen and experienced shocking moments during their tenure. Nothing like the life laid out for Ryan's future back home, sitting in a posh surgery in a well-heeled suburb of Paris filling up a bank vault with euros.

Ryan needed this year off. Needed it badly. He was burnt out. Didn't tell his family that.

Maybe it had been the drug dealing as a young man. The excitement. Fucking dangerous. But it had got to him. All the way. He did love the idea of being a doctor. The 'idea' was motivating . . . at first. But recently he'd had trouble convincing himself that medicine was his calling. Was it only because of family? He hoped not. He needed Médecins Sans Frontières to get him back on track.

The answer was a firm no. There was no part-time work available. He was given a brochure.

'Go onto the website. Sometimes there is something there. Sorry.'

Ryan had been to the website and it stank. No place for a visiting doctor, ex drug dealer.

'I'm not looking to practise here,' he told the woman at the front desk. 'I just want to learn more about the operation from the inside. I could get lunches, coffees.'

'Sorry, we make our own.'

'I'll make it for you.'

'I know how to make my own coffee.'

Ryan stood at the counter thinking of his next move. There was always a next move. Forwards or backwards. He didn't want it to be backwards.

'You can make me one,' came a voice from an inside office. 'Show him how, Anita, and then bring him in here.'

Anita smiled, sort of.

'Follow me.'

And Ryan did. And Ryan met Valerie. Valerie was in charge of the Sydney office. She told Ryan there was no money in it but if he wanted to help out then she had plenty for him. And Ryan became a volunteer. And didn't Ryan love it. Right from the first day Ryan felt he was a contributor even though he did no more than file documents and make coffees. But he was a part of Médecins Sans Frontières and that meant something. To Ryan. Why did it? That was the question he asked himself over and over and over. And the simple answer was 'because I feel good, because I can't wait to go to the office every day'. That would do for now. Went on for three weeks.

Soon he was allowed to sit in on staff meetings. Listen to updates on Afghanistan or Ukraine. Hear of the struggles the children in these countries were facing, how staff were committed to helping. Never wavering. It was impossible not to become personally involved with some stories as they unfolded. Ryan was impressed how the staff kept their emotions in check. It was one foot in front of the other. That's how they got somewhere. It was a lesson.

Ryan thought it was only doctors and nurses that worked with Médecins Sans Frontières, but he learnt early on that the organisation also supplied mechanics and engineers, and of course psychologists. Some field coordinators were required to stay on location for six months at a time. Ryan wondered whether one day he would be brave enough to do six months.

———

Adrian watched the fella walking backwards and forwards around the barn. 'Two fucking dunnies. He's got to be dreaming. And what for? Gonna train the cows to sit on them?'

'How you going to do it?'

The fella calmed down. He looked at Adrian. He so wanted out of this job with the bikies. Six weeks was already tight for getting the barn sorted. And now bloody dunnies.

'Gonna have to get the excavator over here. Gonna have to hire the bloody truck again.'

'What truck?' Adrian asked.

'Bloody truck I used to get the excavator to mine.'

'Had to dig a few big holes at your joint, eh?'

'None of your business.'

'Just asking.'

'Long-drops. One each side. At the end of the barn. Not putting in bloody piping, that's for sure. I guess he'll want them opening into the barn, so we can grab two second-hand doors easy enough. That'll do it. Unless it's for the Queen. Better check.'

The fella laughed at the thought of the Queen using a long-drop.

'He can pay for the truck hire too.'

On the way out the fella stopped the van by the house. Gave a beep. Ace came out and walked over.

'Hey, boys, how's it going. Dunnies in?'

And then he burst out laughing. The fella glared.

'Just a joke. C'mon.'

'We thought we'd build a couple of long-drops. That okay?'

'What's a long-drop?'

'Bloody big hole with a pan sitting over it. Works fine unless you're planning on putting the Queen up.'

This was no joke to Ace.

'Don't matter who it's for, just get it done. Long-drops sound fine.'

'Have to bring my excavator over. It'll cost you.'

'Get the excavator. Dig the holes. And give me my long-drops. Okay? Now piss off.'

And they did. Piss off.

———

Brian had been a good boy. Had no choice. Nolene hadn't taken any business trips since before the party. And she had been very accommodating of his particular desires. Brian was enjoying his newfound sophistication when it came to a 'root'. 'Sexually gratified' and now 'particular desires'. Still nothing wrong with a 'root'.

Nolene was flat out with business. On the phone or at the computer most of the day, seven days a week. They'd been to The Basin a couple of times, late evening after a swim. Brian wasn't all that keen. Didn't fancy coming across Wanda. And of course that thought got him going again. What was it with him and sex these days? Take another swim. Cool down.

'Let's take another swim, darling. So nice in, don't you think?'

'We've only just got out, sweetheart. Let's save it up for tomorrow evening. I've got a special dinner planned for you tonight and I need to get back to prepare it. You'll love it.'

There had been a fair few special dinners lately, and Brian was wondering why.

But tonight's special dinner quickly evaporated with Nolene's phone ringing as they turned into the driveway. She apologised to Brian and took the call into the bedroom.

'You watch telly, sweetheart. Have to take this.'

Special din-dins changed to tomorrow.

'You don't mind, do you? That's my boy.'

Brian turned the telly onto *The Bachelor* and made a toastie.

———

Nolene had dreaded the call. Dreaded it because it was thrilling but also because of the probable consequences. She had

been flat out for the past few years with work and conferences. Conferences. That's where they start, don't they?
People thrown together for a weekend. Dinners. Drinks.
Work. Fun. And then a second and third conference and
re-engaging with some of the same people. And then looking
forward to re-engaging with the same people. And then. And
then of course it was going to happen. Why had she been
kidding herself? He was great company. And smart. And
admiring. And so they ended up in the sack. 'Never again,'
they both said. That was until the next conference, when
she almost raced for the bed on arrival. Guilty. That's what
she felt. Very fucking guilty. Poor Brian at home working
himself stupid selling properties while she was shagging the
senior sales rep of a lingerie company. And trying the stuff
on. Christ. And so she decided 'no more' and that she would
make it up to Brian big time. And now Mr Ladies Lingerie
was on the phone.

And Mr Ladies Lingerie is wanting her to tell her
husband that she has another conference and to meet him
in Melbourne for a dirty weekend. And Nolene is finding it
hard to say no.

———

Sheila couldn't work him out. She'd made it pretty obvious
that she was keen, but either Adrian was as slow as a wet
week or he wasn't interested. He'd certainly seemed interested after the party, in the park. His hands were everywhere,
as were hers. Since then, nothing. She never saw him when
she came to clean. He left her eighty bucks on the kitchen
table. Must have left early for whatever he was working on,

because she was there by seven-thirty. And she had spruced up her act for him, if he'd bothered to be there to notice. Bit frillier. Saucier. Easier to get at or under or over.

He was a funny bugger, Adrian was. Been in the area for just over six months. He had a personality. Cheeky and ironic. She'd tried to get some background out of him but he was a bit secretive about the past, so she didn't push it. The house didn't give anything away either. And she looked. Opened a few drawers. Checked his desk. Clean as. This made him even more attractive to Sheila. Let her imagination run riot. On the run from the cops? Fugitive hiding out? But he was definitely not hiding out. He went to a bloody party. Groped her in the park. Getting over a bad relationship? Yep, that made sense. A shithouse divorce and not keen on getting involved too soon. That was fine with Sheila. She could wait.

29

The fella had told Adrian to take the morning off while he organised the excavator. Really shat the fella off now having to build two dunnies. And hire a truck and cart the bloody thing over to the bikies' joint. Pain in the arse.

Adrian took advantage of the break to whip into Coffs Harbour. He could get a meeting if the 9 am flight arriving from Sydney would work for him. And it did. They went to the jetty. Found a place to sit and feed the seagulls while they talked and had coffee. Pretty private. He was told the bikes were registered to addresses in south-west Sydney. Two of the bikies had form. Andrew Mullens, known as Ace, and Donald Mitchell.

Adrian gave a rundown on the race to finish the barn. Said he'd hopefully have more news soon. Reckoned things were heating up. That was the info coming through. Preparing for a cargo and movement. They finished the meeting in time for the 11.30 am return flight to Sydney and in time for Adrian to get back and be picked up by the fella for a few hours' afternoon work on the barn.

———

Sergeant Gallagher was pleased the bottle shop owner had come round and agreed to the deal with Wayne. The kid had been foolish but there wasn't badness in the kid. His grandmother Moira jumped on him big time. Scary one, that Moira. Wouldn't want her coming after you. Sergeant Gallagher couldn't see the boy acting up again. It was great how it worked now down at the Legal Service. Elders and previous offenders brought in to talk to the boys when they broke the law. Tell them their stories and how grateful they were they didn't end up back inside.

The sergeant's job was to uphold the law, but that wasn't as easy as it sounded. Not a lot of bank robberies these days or house break-ins. Sure, kids did some mischief looking for a bit of excitement but a good smack over the ear or a conversation on what they could expect once they were inside usually sorted them out. Jail isn't nice.

There was weed growing out the back there in places. Vietnamese gangs seemed to control it. Built igloos that could hold ten thousand plants. And the Vietnamese were non-violent. If caught they'd move their workers, who were all in Australia on work visas, off to another plantation, sometimes on the other side of the country. But that sort of crime was handled by the Drug Squad. Sometimes local cops might help but mostly you just passed on anything suspicious.

Domestic violence incidents took up most of the local cops' time. And dealing with the media, who were always telling you that you'd gone in too hard or too soft. Bloody hard to win. Still, Sergeant Gallagher wouldn't want any other job. Wouldn't mind a bank robbery though. Up the excitement.

It had to be over two weeks since she'd been snatched. Grabbed. Kidnapped. Stolen. Had to be. But she had survived it. That she knew. God, she'd had to dig deep and yes, sometimes she begged a god, if one existed. Leila had to believe. She had to believe someone would help her. She took on the voice. The voice that told her she would die here or be killed here. She took it on. She knew about the voice. Pretending it was her friend but trying to take her down, down into darkness. She knew she could give in to it or fight it.

Leila was a fighter.

'I'm a fighter.'

She screamed it.

And then she would cry. Until one day she stopped crying and knew she had beaten the voice.

He came to her every day, always bringing food and water. He made her eat and smiled when she refused to eat. Like when she threw the food against the wall. She learnt not to do that. No win in that.

But as the days passed he started to treat her differently. He would sit on the bed beside her and tell her what his day had been like and ask her what her day had been like. Leila didn't have a clue how to answer. She'd mumble stuff.

'Went for a walk . . . around the room.'

'Good, good,' he'd say.

'Barn's going well,' he'd tell her. 'Roof's nearly covered.'

And then he'd leave.

Once Leila was given the clock, things changed. The clock was important. It helped with routine. For some ten hours at a time she was on her own. It was just her and the room.

Back when she had been in rehab with her broken back, Leila had learnt about herself. She had learnt how to deal with herself. Leila had always been impatient. Always wanting to move quickly on to the next thing, whatever that was. Work or fun. But with a broken back there was no moving on quickly. She learnt the answer to moving on was sticking to the rehab routine, because the rehab determined when she would be healed, not her impatience.

That's where the clock came in. She could set her day. She would need to stick to it. She would accept the moment. Nothing lasts. In time she would be free. That's what lay in front of Leila. She wasn't scared of him. He wanted her alive. And alive she would be when they came for her.

And so her day would begin. Wake. Wash. Wait for him. Eat. She would thank him for her food and ask him what he had planned for his day. How was his work progressing? She knew she had to be a part of whatever crazy fantasy he had created for her. She was his.

Yoga was important. Meditation was a fight. Too damn easy to drift off. Had to keep pulling herself back to the moment. Not easy. Easy for the wellness gurus. But they weren't being held captive in a fucking room. Maybe it should be a requirement for every wellness guru to go through that. Being held captive. Then they might not be so smug.

Leila forced herself to remember books she had read. Films she had seen. Like *Papillon*. She now was Papillon.

And then he would return. Ask her to lie on the bed with him and put her arms around him.

'It's alright, I'm here,' Leila would say.

Did she dare say that Mummy was here? She tried it.

'Mummy is here. It's okay.'

And she waited. Waited. Waited.

The fella looked at her. Would he bash her?

'Are you hungry?'

'Yes.'

And then he brought her food.

—

At the end of one day the fella appeared with a long rope. He asked Leila to stand. He tied the rope around Leila's neck.

'We're going out. You will be good, won't you?'

Leila nodded. Her heart thumped. She was going outside. She would see where she was.

He opened the door. There were stairs. He walked up the stairs. Leila followed. The rope around her neck. Then they stepped out into a yard. Leila looked back at the stairs. She had no idea she had been in a room under the house. Leila looked up at the sky. It had never looked so good. She wanted to cry at its beauty. A sky she had taken for granted every day of her young life.

He walked Leila to a fire pit with logs placed around it. There was a table set up with food. The fire pit had a hotplate attached to a steel rod sitting over it.

He took two steaks and placed them on the hotplate. There was a billy boiling to which he added frozen peas.

Leila looked around. There was a shack beside the

stairwell, obviously where the fella lived, and a shed just opposite. No other houses in sight. Just bush. Leila knew she should be scared but she wasn't. She was unusually calm.

He cut the steak for her. Put it on a plate and added peas. He gave her a spoon.

He watched as Leila ate.

'Good, eh?'

'Very.'

When she had finished, he took the plate and spoon and handed her a glass of water. Leila drank from the glass.

'Want to go for a drive?'

Leila stared at the fella. He was going to take her for a drive. Was this coming to an end? Could it be true?

'Please.'

He led her by the rope to the shed. Opened the shed. And there was a car. An old car. Leila hadn't seen a car like it before. Not in Denmark.

He opened the passenger side door and told Leila to get in. Then he went around and got into the driver's seat.

They sat there, Leila looking across at him.

'Shut your eyes.'

Leila shut her eyes.

'We're going to the beach.'

Leila waited for the engine to turn over.

'Are you enjoying the drive?'

And Leila knew she was going nowhere. Tears began to run down her cheeks. She dug deep.

'Yes, it's lovely.'

She opened her eyes and looked at the fella. His eyes were shut and he was smiling.

After the drive, he took Leila back to the bunker and lay down with her.

This then became their evening. Dinner and a drive. To nowhere.

'Let's drive across the country,' she said. 'I'd love to see the outback.'

'Close your eyes,' he'd say.

And then they would drive across the outback.

———

He used the excavator to dig holes on each side of the barn. Planks were placed across the holes, leaving a smaller opening for the toilet pans to cover. Long drops. Doorways were cut into the sides of the barn and framing erected for the outhouses. They had plenty of gal for the outhouse roofing. The barn roof was almost done. Good strong beams and new gal covering them. The walls were coming along, but now windows were to be added. High up and with a wire grille. There was to be no glass. Some sort of shutter would do. The electrics weren't in too bad a shape and they soon had the lights working fine.

The fella kept asking Adrian what he thought the barn was to be used for. Why would a shipment of drugs need a dunny, or fucking two? The fella wondered.

He was keen to get the excavator home and return the truck, so he set off at smoko. Told Adrian to get the windows in. He'd be back to pick Adrian up early afternoon.

'Not a problem,' Adrian told the fella.

Not a problem at all because Adrian had been wanting a chance to snoop. On their drive in, passing the house, they'd seen a couple of large tarpaulins covering something. Adrian was keen to know what the something was. Better have an excuse if he was caught snooping.

Bloody bad headache. That would be the excuse.

Adrian worked until midday, then took a wander down to the house. Pit bulls were around and the bikes, but no four-wheel. Adrian wandered to the something and lifted a tarp.

The pit bulls began barking.

Adrian dropped the tarp and continued to the house. The door to the house opened and the third bikie came out with a shotgun aimed at Adrian's guts.

'What the fuck are you doin'?'

'Crook, mate. Splittin' fuckin' headache and GT has taken the truck back. I need a fuckin' Panadol. You got any, mate?'

The bikie stared hard at Adrian. Walked to him. Shoved the gun into Adrian's chest.

'This should cure your fuckin' headache.'

'Careful, mate. That thing might go off.'

'You blokes were told to stay out at the barn.'

'I know that, mate, but fair dinkum it's killin' me. You got any Panadol? Then I can get on with the work.'

The bikie stayed looking at Adrian. Then lowered the shotgun.

'Wait here.'

And Adrian did until the bikie came out with a couple of Panadol.

He handed them to Adrian.

'Got some water?'

'Use the tap at the barn. Now piss off.'

And Adrian did.

Adrian now knew what the something was under the tarps. Mattresses. At least a dozen of them. Well used.

The fella dropped Adrian home early arvo. He had come back after dropping off the excavator and truck. Said he'd had enough. Running around tires a bloke out. Said he needed to get home and rest up. He was resting up a bit this past week. Knockoff was more like two-thirty than three, but starts were getting earlier too.

The fella couldn't wait to get home to be with her. His her. He was sure she liked seeing him.

He drove home and locked the gates behind him. Didn't really need to lock them. Who the fuck was going to come out here? Intrude on their time. But you never knew, so lock up.

He parked the van and went inside. Washed up like she had taught him. He went to the fridge and grabbed tonight's meat. T-bones. He knew she'd like T-bones. There would be veg too. Got to eat your veg, she had always said. Bung it all in together straight into the frypan. Bloody delicious.

The fella took the food out to the pit. She loved it out here, he knew that. Loved going for a drive. So did he. It was the best. He wondered where she might like to go today. Maybe the Blue Mountains. Dave took his mum there in the old days. These were new days.

He placed the food on the table by the pit, checking he had enough wood, and then went to the trapdoor. He couldn't wait to see her. He walked down the stairs and opened the wooden door and there she was, sitting on the side of the bed smiling at him. He took the rope he had hanging by the door and then opened the grille door. She stood as he approached her and tied the rope around her neck. Then he led Leila out of the bunker, up the stairs and out into the yard.

Leila sat on the ground while he lit the fire and placed the food in the frypan. Their dinner would be ready very soon and then off to the Blue Mountains. He wondered if she had been to the Blue Mountains. Probably not, but you never knew with these backpackers. They did get about.

Drinks time. Treat time. Tonight would be a treat. It would be a treat giving her Coca-Cola.

He went into the house. As he opened the fridge sitting by the window, there was a flash. A reflection. Where the hell did that come from? Looked through the window. Nothing.

Quietly he moved to the back of the house. Grabbed a rope. Climbed out a window and crouched. The fella moved slowly to the corner of the house and looked. Still nothing. And then he saw him. A kid lying in the grass under a gum tree by the shed. The kid was looking towards the front of the house. He had a phone in his hand. It was the sun shining off the kid's phone that made the flash.

The fella leant in the window and grabbed one of the plastic shopping bags lying on the floor, then crept along the side of the dam to the back of the shed. The boy was only a couple of metres from him. Who was this fucking kid? How dare he be here? And with that thought he slammed the bag over the kid's head. The kid struggled, trying to breathe through the plastic. He was no match for the fella. The fella wound the rope around the kid's arms and dragged him to the dam and held his head underwater until the struggling stopped.

A three-quarter moon hung from the sky.

Nolene didn't know how to break the news to Brian. She knew he would be disappointed about her going away again. But her colleague was insistent. 'Colleague' sounded more professional. Made her feel less guilty than 'lover'. She didn't like herself for what she was doing. Going to Melbourne for a dirty weekend. Perhaps a day or two longer. What did that make it? A dirty long weekend.

She needed to be down there by the end of the week was what she told Brian. It was an important business meeting. Might lead to a top business transaction for the company. Who was she kidding? Since when had she become such a good liar? Her poor Brian. He would be grief-stricken if he knew. This would be the last time. That's why she was going down, to tell her colleague 'no more'. The end. Full stop. Just one more fucking and that was it.

Her poor Brian hardly heard any of the explanation about it being good for the company. As soon as Nolene mentioned she was off to Melbourne, all he could think of was Wanda. Like how could he avoid her? Like hell. There was no way Brian was going to avoid seeing Wanda. No siree. Give the van a really good clean-out. That's what he'd do. Maybe spray a little something nice in it. She'd appreciate that. That wasn't all she'd appreciate.

Brian couldn't wait for the weekend. Neither could Nolene.

30

It was three days since David's funeral and Sergeant Gallagher still had that nag. David's bike hadn't turned up. None of his mates had it or had any idea where it might be. The nag kept getting bigger but what to do about it? And the kid's clothes. Why hadn't they been found? All of this added to the nag. Wasn't going away, that's for sure.

It was the nag brought the sarge to The Basin. That was the hangout. That's where the goss operated from. He didn't really know what he expected by going there, but he had learnt to trust his instincts. They'd been wrong plenty of times but that didn't mean he gave up on them. Anyway, a lunchtime coffee wouldn't go astray.

The sarge didn't surf, not that he didn't wish he did. Most blokes on the coast surfed or had surfed. Same with weed. Most smoked or had smoked. That wasn't one of his wishes. He remembered the party where he'd smoked a joint. Fact is he didn't remember the party. Just got told he was there. He'd ended up falling asleep by the railway line. Stationmaster came down, told him train drivers were reporting a body by the tracks. Did he want to get himself killed? No, thank you. Never again.

The sarge ordered his coffee and took a seat looking out at the park. There were a couple of locals doing the same.

'Mind if I join you?'

He turned to find the rather attractive Wanda smiling at him.

'Nope, please do.'

And that was how the sarge and Wanda ended up spending a couple of hours together discussing David's death and funeral.

Wanda thought the funeral was one of the most beautiful services she'd ever experienced. It was soulful. That was the word. Wanda had never used soulful before. Too wanky, she reckoned. She'd heard enough about the soul at school. Over and over and over. But she couldn't think of a better word for the funeral. She wasn't sure if it was because of the words or the music or the way the funeral was held. The location. The day. It was soulful. Yep, soulful. She mustn't go on about it, she thought. Okay. Soulful.

The sarge told Wanda about the nag he had about David's bike not turning up. He'd done an extensive search centred around the three-kilometre mark for the bike and David's clothes but nothing. Of course, David might have gone in for a swim anywhere, but he had hoped they'd come across something. He'd also hoped one of the locals might have seen something. Might have noticed David at the beach late in the day. But no. No sightings.

Wanda knew she needed to talk to Brian about the van

they'd passed on the way back from their dalliance. Their dalliance in the back of Brian's van with her head on a saddle. The sarge's nag was now becoming Wanda's nag. There was probably nothing to it, but it was a van that night and it was going to the three-kilometre mark. What if it had some connection to David's death? Of course it didn't, but she knew she should mention it. And so the Pandora's box was opened. She said she didn't want to name the man she was with but she told the sarge as much as she could remember. What she had seen.

Told him it must have been a little before 9 pm and that it was a van and that it had been travelling to the three-kilometre mark. She couldn't see who was driving as the headlights were in her eyes. It was definitely a van, she was sure of that. Maybe white. And that was about all she could say.

The sarge asked if she'd seen the van before. Wanda said there were always vans around the beach. Surfers loved them.

And then of course the sarge asked who Wanda was with on the night. Wanda begged him not to force her to reveal her companion but she knew there was no turning back now. Pandora's box was wide open.

'It was Brian Slaviero, Sarge.'

The sarge thanked Wanda and guaranteed he would be discreet in his questioning of Brian. Hopefully there was no reason to bring Brian's wife into this. Most likely the van had nothing to do with David's death, but he'd need to check it out.

Wanda knew she needed to contact Brian and explain. Knew he wouldn't exactly be happy about her conversation with the sarge. She excused herself and left The Basin.

Sergeant Gallagher ordered another coffee and called Benny over. The sarge had been contacted by Missing Persons to check out the disappearance of a young Danish woman called Leila Sodahl. Leila's parents had been in touch with the Danish authorities as they hadn't heard from their daughter in over a month. They were worried. Her texts were as regular as clockwork. Leila's last text gave The Basin on the east coast of Australia as her whereabouts. It was where she was waitressing.

Benny enthused over Leila. Told the sarge she was a great worker and had easily made herself part of the local scene. She was well liked by the locals and totally reliable until she took off.

'Don't know what we'd do without the backpackers. Love 'em.'

'Thank God for our backpackers, Sarge.'

Benny said it was a shame to lose Leila and had no idea where she'd moved on to.

'They come and go. Move with the tides or the romances.' He laughed. 'I reckon that's what happened to Leila. She was a pretty good-looking young girl.'

'Notice any romances?'

'Nope, didn't, which is why I was a little surprised when she left. Just up and went. Still, it's happened before and it'll happen again.'

Benny explained Conchita's party had continued till late and that Leila was great and stayed on to help tidy. She had the Sunday off but was due back the following day.

'She didn't show up. Cleared out from her accommodation leaving dough for the cleaning. Moved on.'

And that was about all Benny could tell the sarge.

'Maybe Brian Slaviero, the estate agent, could tell you more. He rented her the apartment.'

The sarge was pleased to get that bit of info seeing as it gave him another excuse to talk to Brian.

———

Wanda texted Brian.

'Need to talk.'

Brian was very, very happy to receive Wanda's text. Nolene had left that morning for another trip to Melbourne and Brian was all by his lonesome. Not for long, it looked like.

'Let's get together this evening. I'm fancy free.'

The reply made him even happier.

'Now.'

———

'You what? You told the fucking sergeant we were together? Are you fucking joking? It will be all over the fucking town in ten seconds. Shit, what am I going to tell Nolene? Fuck. Fuck. Fuck.'

'Calm down, lover boy. The sarge just wants a few words and he's promised to be discreet.'

They were sitting in Brian's van down by the beach. Wanda placed her hand on Brian's thigh. Squeezed.

'So Missus Slav's away, eh?'

'Yeah. Shit, why'd you tell him?'

'Had to. He's still trying to work out what happened to David, the boy that drowned.'

'He drowned.'

'Maybe. The sarge has a nag. Needs to get rid of it. Do you have a nag, Brian?'

And Wanda squeezed Brian's thigh again. Brian did have a nag and it was getting bigger. Couldn't think straight with Wanda's hand on his thigh. And Brian had to think this through. Sergeant Gallagher wanted a word with him about the night before a boy's body was found washed up on the beach. He thought hard about it. There was nothing he could tell the sarge that might help explain the boy's death. Yes, he and Wanda had passed a van that night, but so what? He didn't see the van properly, so what could he add? He could add, of course, that he was having it off with a local in the back of his van while his wife was away. Something he wasn't proud of. Or was he? Sure, he'd enjoyed the encounter, but no, he wasn't proud of it. Where did the word 'encounter' come from? He was losing it big time. He and Wanda had had it off in the back of his van. That was the story, and if Nolene found out she'd cut off his balls. It mustn't get out. Brian needed to get on the front foot and speak to Sergeant Gallagher immediately. That's what Brian told Wanda he was going to do.

But Wanda had her hand on Brian's thigh and kept squeezing it. Wanda wondered, only wondered, mind you, if maybe it wouldn't be better to talk to the sarge tomorrow. Brian would still be on the front foot. That was a pretty good idea, Wanda thought, because it meant she could be on her back tonight.

Wanda gave Brian's thigh another squeeze just as there was a knock on the window of Brian's van.

Brian freaked when he turned and saw a smiling Sergeant Gallagher. He wound down the window.

'Hi, Sergeant. I was about to come looking for you. Wanda told me you wanted a word.'

'Yep, Brian, sure do. Do you mind stepping out of your van?'

And that's what Brian Slaviero did. Very obediently stepped out of his van to answer questions about the night before David was found dead.

———

The sergeant poured himself a beer. Into a glass. Reckoned that's how a beer should be drunk. You needed to see the head. He stared at the head of the beer and thought. Something wasn't right. That bloody nag would kill him.

Brian was close to useless about the night. But there had been a van driving to the three-kilometre mark, that was for certain. They had both seen it. Maybe white. Wanda was right about vans on the coast. Everywhere. But where was this van now? That's what was on the sarge's mind.

And the Danish girl, Leila Sodahl. What was that all about? Just pissing off. No please or thank you, 'just out of here'. Of course, that happens with the backpackers. They're on holiday and going with the flow. But that nag was developing into a problem nag for the sarge. Benny was certainly surprised by her leaving. It was out of her nature he felt. If you can get anybody's nature in five weeks.

The sarge downed his beer. Got another. They couldn't be related, could they? David's death and Leila's disappearance? Three weeks apart. Seemed bloody unlikely, however the sarge had learned the more unlikely something seemed the more likely it was it happened.

The link was Brian. Tenuous at best. Brian had sorted the girl out with accommodation and collected the cleaning money. And Brian saw a van. Unrelated, surely.

A third beer wouldn't help so the sarge didn't have it. Tomorrow he'd let Missing Persons know he'd investigated Leila's disappearance and found nothing. That wouldn't satisfy her parents. He hoped Missing Persons would tell the parents that in most cases the missing person shows up. But not in all cases. Shit a brick. Alright then, he'd investigate further.

That's what you're supposed to do as a cop. Investigate. One thing he did know was that he'd put the fear of God into Brian. Brian was terrified the sarge would tell Nolene he was playing 'hide the sausage' with Wanda. Who thinks up these sayings? Sarge was told it's the crims inside think up the really bad shit. Couldn't give a stuff about the world that didn't give a stuff about them. Could be true, the sarge reckoned as he called it a night.

———

It was pretty much done and looked bloody good. Definitely wouldn't fall over in a gale or even a cyclone. Not that they had cyclones on this part of the coast. The fella had found a bunch of shutters at a recycling centre. Only needed a bit of work to make them fit the barn windows. He got Adrian to do that while he worked out what they were owed. The bikies were no slouches when it came to paying. Never an argument and always paid in cash. Didn't get any better than that. Came to about twenty-five grand all up. And now the fella was getting the last five.

As Ace counted the five grand into the fella's hand, the fella asked a stupid question. He knew it was stupid as he asked it.

'So what you gonna use it for? The barn.'

Yep, stupid.

Ace looked fair into the face of the fella.

'It's none of your fucking business. And more than that, you wipe any memory of what you been doing here right out of that dim-witted fucking mind of yours. Got it? That goes for your mate too. Never happened, right?'

The fella was only too happy to assure Ace that he had not only never worked on the barn but that he'd never laid eyes on any of the bikies. Not ever.

Then Ace slapped his arm around the fella and said, 'Good job, GT. Now get your mate and fuck off.'

And that's what the fella did. He went and got Adrian. Packed the van. And vamoosed.

———

The fella dropped Adrian back home. They chatted about the weirdo bikies and what the barn was for. The fella was sure it was for drugs. Thought maybe it would be a lab. Meth labs were being set up in houses up the coast, he knew that. He gave Adrian his outstanding wages.

'When do you think Benny will take some more weed?'

Adrian batted him away, told him the cops were still fiddling with the drowning.

'Won't be long. I'll let you know.'

Adrian shook the fella's hand.

'Thanks for the job, mate. Came in handy. We should catch up for a beer once things have settled.'

'Yeah, sure,' said the fella and then revved up the van and took off. As he drove past The Basin he passed Brian in his van. Brian waved.

———

The bikies stood looking at the barn. They were impressed.

'Knew what they were doin'.'

'Told you they'd come through, Don.'

Ace was feeling very pleased with himself. And relieved. Time was running out. Word had come down that the first of the cargo was about to leave. They had work to do.

31

The day came for Anna to get the bus. There were hugs all round. Kisses all round. Tears all round. Manuel brooded but wished her luck and carried her suitcase onto the bus.

She would text them all on arrival in Australia.

Anna had caught the bus to São Paulo a few times over the years to see the cousins. This time was different. She looked out the bus window at the scenery she would not see again for a while. Maybe ever, if she decided to stay in Australia. Who knows? Maybe she would marry one of the tall good-looking Australians she saw on social media.

José met Anna at the bus station. She threw her arms around him. He took her suitcase. She had never been happier. Her plane was leaving that night at eight o'clock. Plenty of time to get to the migration agency and have her visa stamped onto her passport. Anna thought José was a genius. How lucky was she to have met him? It was meant to be.

The agency's office was down a back street near the bus terminal. José took Anna's passport and told her to wait. Her heart was thumping. What if they declined her visa? Anna would die, she believed. But they didn't decline her visa. José passed the passport to Anna to see. There was the visa to work in Australia. She looked at José and tears streamed down her face. José the hero. Her hero.

And now her hero was taking her to lunch on Oscar Freire to enjoy *moqueca*. Anna loved fish stew. It was her favourite. They toasted Anna's trip with a caipirinha. Only the one, because Anna had no intention of missing her flight. She was being very careful. This was her trip of a lifetime.

She asked José if they could visit the Sé Cathedral, the most beautiful cathedral in São Paulo. Anna needed to thank God for this opportunity to help her family. This opportunity to live a new life.

She knelt in front of the statue of the Virgin Mary. She bowed her head and prayed. She asked for humility and grace to be the girl she was but enjoy the riches that might come her way. She smiled up at the statue. This was not a time for tears.

For the next two hours they walked the streets of São Paulo. Anna asked if she might take José's arm. She wished to be a beautiful girl on the arm of a handsome man, like other couples walking the streets of São Paulo.

At five in the evening José hailed a taxi to take them to São Paulo–Guarulhos International Airport. Anna could hardly sit still with excitement. The taxi seemed to take forever. So many cars, so many people.

As they neared the airport Anna became anxious again. Was this the right thing to do? Was she just a stupid young naive girl? José could see her worry. Such a gentleman. He took her hand and told her all was fine and that she was on the trip of a lifetime. He told her there would be other young girls on the plane on their way to Australia for a new life just like her.

The taxi dropped them at the airport terminal and José carried Anna's bag to the line for her departure. He had told Anna she would be met in Sydney by his very good friend Lucas. He had a photograph of his very good friend and showed it to Anna.

'He's very reliable and will look after you. Nothing to worry about. He's helped many South American girls like you in search of a wonderful new life.'

Anna was next up at the counter. Her passport was checked and her suitcase taken. It was now time to say goodbye and pass through security. Anna thanked José and gave him a hug.

'I will never forget you, José.'

José wished her well as she headed to security. When Anna looked back to wave, José was nowhere to be seen.

———

The inside of the plane was so big. Anna looked around for other girls like her whose lives were about to change. There were some and Anna smiled at those girls but there were no smiles back. Silly girls. They should show their happiness. The plane was taking them to their Wonderland. Up, up and away.

Adrian met the 4.40 pm flight from Sydney. He was sitting having coffee in the airport cafeteria when his supervisor arrived. His supervisor was flying back at ten past six, so no time to head out. It was private. Place was empty but for them.

The word was the operation was on. Seems the first of the cargo was on its way.

'So where are we?'

'We're good, barn's finished. Said our goodbyes.'

The bloke gave Adrian the plan. He was to keep an eye on the place.

'Can you find an excuse to go back? Get a sense of the urgency. Numbers would be good.'

'What, and get myself shot? They aren't mucking around, mate.'

'Can you get near the place? Take some shots of arrivals?'

'I can try.'

Adrian saw the bloke onto the six-ten to Sydney. His adrenaline was starting to run.

———

Adrenaline running. That was a sign. A sign he was about to strike trouble. Which he used to long for. Early on. Hopefully that was in the past because he had more sense now. He hoped. My god he hoped that was the case.

It got bad after his dad was killed. Really bad. Grog and drugs. Menial work. Hard menial work, but he could have aimed higher. Higher than the gutter where he ended up. Blowing every cent he made and borrowed, on horses and pokies and cards and any other opportunity where he could show he was the self-pitying fuckwit he'd become. Didn't take long. Crying into the arms of a mate who led him to a TAB and showed him the drain. Grog and drugs had to follow. You need something to convince yourself you're a victim. And then after ten years in this gutter he bumped into one of his dad's best cop mates. Staggered into him in a lane, off his head, while his dad's best cop mate was busting an illegal gambling haunt. Someone who really cared about him as him, not as a victim.

The hand of friendship went out. A sobering followed and then two years down the track the chance to do what his dad did. Become a cop. Did he have the balls? He had to have the balls. It was that or perish. Thus Adrian the cop. And then Adrian the undercover cop. Of course. He had the absolute credentials. And now this posting up the coast, six months ago, because word had gone out. Shit was happening up there and a nose was needed. Adrian had a good nose. He smelled out the fella, didn't he? The weed was little stuff, but who knows where that might lead. Certainly not to this, that's for sure. But it has and it's big stuff. Big dirty stuff. Gutter stuff. And Adrian has the inside. And the adrenaline is running. Not running away this time. He's on top of it and intends to deliver. Adrian knows there's intel from an informer. The bloke has hinted at it in the meetings. Adrian wonders who. No point wondering. He's been given an assignment. Adrenaline's running. Thought he might get in touch with Sheila and see how her adrenaline was running.

———

Wanda couldn't sleep. The sarge's nag had got into her dreams. Same dream over and over. David screaming for help in the ocean and surfers paddling past telling him to swim. They wouldn't do that, of course. Not the surfers she knew. It had to be her subconscious telling her that David's death was being ignored.

Wanda had been up for an hour with her notebook. This was the opportunity. No puff piece. This would be a powerful piece telling the story of a boy drowning in suspicious circumstances and how a town needed to stand up and not ignore this death. She liked the idea for the story. It would be about the coast and the people and the Indigenous population. The history of colonisation in the area and the destruction of the Indigenous community. The story would be the backdrop to the death of David. She needed to speak to David's family. Wanda needed depth to the piece. She was excited. Maybe her article could help expose the reason for David's death. If there was a reason outside of a young kid being stupid enough to go for a night swim in the ocean.

The sarge's surprise turn-up at the van the day before had cooled any chance of romance with Brian. It was pretty obvious that she might be waiting a while to get into the back of Brian's van after the sarge's intervention. Even with a few more squeezes of Brian's thigh. No, not tonight, Josephine, whoever Josephine was. Brian was shaken. Two things in particular had shaken him. The first was that the sarge knew he'd been cheating on Nolene. Now that that genie was out of the bottle, he thought it was sure to get to Nolene eventually. Wanda had told Brian not to be so paranoid.

The sarge had said he would be discreet. Didn't help. Brian was shitting himself. And the second was that Brian had lied at the earlier questioning straight after David's death, saying he'd seen nothing. Had gone home early after an inspection. He'd lied to a cop.

Brian had apologised and offered to drop Wanda home. Wanda had thanked him and told him to get a good night's rest. She'd walk. All will be better in the morning, she'd told him. Wanda needed the walk. A chance to think. She'd been surprised that the sarge was still investigating the boy's death. Seemed like it was done and dusted. Death by drowning. No suspicious circumstances. That wasn't how the sarge saw it. He had a nag. And now Wanda had a story. Maybe. Needed to convince the *Courier* and then needed help. Someone trusted, to meet David's family. If it was going to be any sort of decent article she needed some inside. Inside on the family and history of the area. Not white history. Black history.

She knew who could help. Would he help? Different matter. She'd convince him. That's what journos do. Convince. Not badger. Ken would be paid a visit at the Legal Service the next day. How could he say no? He'd want justice to be done. Presuming there'd been an injustice.

Wanda was getting excited. She was now convinced an injustice had been done. Only taken an hour. And with these thoughts Wanda took herself back to bed. But not to sleep.

———

Adrian yawned awake. Hands behind head and thinking. And smiling. There was a reason for the smile and the reason lay beside him. Sheila. Her adrenaline had indeed been running, and an invitation to join her for dinner was offered. He obliged.

There was more on his mind, of course. The bikies and the next step. His supervisor had wanted more. Wanted Adrian to keep an eye on the place and report back on any 'movement at the station'.

Adrian was a fan of the poem, 'The Man from Snowy River'. His father knew it by heart and would often proclaim it after a couple of beers.

> There was movement at the station, for the word had
>> passed around
> That the colt from Old Regret had got away,
> And had joined the wild bush horses . . .

Thinking about his dad made Adrian emotional. About the only thing that did. It also reminded him that his dad went all the way. No slacker. Same for Adrian. Gonna nail the bikie scum.

Sheila moved into him.

'Don't think this means you get your cleaning done for free.'

Adrian smiled at her. Touched her lips.

'Maybe a slight discount for services rendered,' she said.

'Maybe, but I'll need to sample a little more to be sure.'

Yep, it was still dark. A further sample wouldn't go astray before he hit the road.

———

At 7.30 am Wanda parked opposite Ken's house. She hadn't got a wink in since she went back to bed, so instead of hitting the Aboriginal Legal Service and catching Ken at work she'd decided to get him before work. And now she was out front.

The door opened and Conchita came out. Ken was seeing her off. A lingering kiss between the two of them made Wanda smile. Good for you, Conchita girl, she thought. Glad someone's getting their rocks off. Then Conchita hopped into her car and waved goodbye to Ken. Obviously had a good night, the pair of them, Wanda reckoned.

Ken returned inside the house, shutting his door. Wanda figured it was her turn so a walk up the drive and a knock on the door saw a startled Ken answering.

'Nope, not your girlfriend,' offered Wanda.

'And to what do I owe this pleasure so early in the day?' replied Ken.

And Wanda told him how she intended to write an article on David and needed help with an intro to the family. Ken listened and then told Wanda he'd meet her for coffee in twenty at The Basin.

At eight in the morning The Basin is alive with locals. Three demographics are obvious.

Surfers. Workers. Non-workers. The latter consisting of retirees, the unemployed and the underemployed. Wanda knew most there and shouted out a number of 'hellos'. She settled on a stool by the window looking out at the park, making sure she kept a stool for Ken.

Ken was no slouch, turning up on the dot twenty minutes later.

'You got me on the right day. Late start.'

'Made late by your girlfriend or intended late start?'

'Does it matter? You got me.'

And so Wanda and Ken reopened the conversation on Wanda's determination to do an article on David.

Ken wasn't against the idea but was unsure he could help, telling Wanda the family was still grieving. Wanda explained the sarge had a nag and was pressing on with inquiries.

'What if there was foul play? Shouldn't we help get to the bottom of it? An article in the *Courier* might stir the possum.'

Wanda wasn't wrong, Ken knew that. Too often the death or disappearance of an Indigenous kid is hardly investigated. He'd seen it too many times. Far too many times. Why it had happened before was to do with latent racism. Ken was sure of that. Couldn't let it continue.

Ken told Wanda he would have a chat with the family. With Moira and Wayne, and get back to her.

'I'll do my best, but don't hold your breath.'

'Thanks, Ken. I promise I'll be respectful and sensitive. No sensationalising. I mean it.'

'I trust you.'

Wanda leant over and kissed Ken on the cheek.

32

Anna was tired. Very, very tired. She had left São Paulo at ten-thirty at night and it was now fifty-one hours later. Her watch showed São Paulo time. One-thirty am. The pilot announced the arrival time in Sydney as two-thirty in the afternoon. She had been travelling for two whole days. No—more! How far away was this Australia?

There had been so many stops and changes of aeroplane. First was Chicago, then Nevada, and then Los Angeles and then Fiji. She could have been landing on the moon. Sydney seemed so far away. And at each stop she'd had to wait hours before boarding the next aeroplane. One time for five hours. Anna thought José must have spent a great deal of money arranging so difficult a trip and couldn't wait to be able to pay him back from the wages she would earn fruit picking.

As the plane landed, Anna felt her excitement grow. She had stamped on her brain the face of José's friend she was to meet. Couldn't wait to see him. The plane slowly taxied to the terminal. As it stopped, people jumped up to get their bags, so eager she thought to get to Australia. Anna looked around for the young girl she had seen on the aeroplane at São Paulo. She'd noticed her at a couple of the other stop-overs and had wanted to introduce herself but thought what an idiot she would appear if the young girl was only visiting relatives or actually lived in Australia.

With people clogging the aisle it was taking forever to empty. Children and the elderly didn't make it any easier. They should file off first, Anna thought. If she ran the airline that's how she would handle it. Children and elderly first.

And now suddenly Anna was out of the aeroplane. She couldn't stop smiling as she waited in the queue to show her passport. The line was long and it took some fifteen minutes to reach the official at the desk. The official looked at the passport then turned to the visa and then to her computer, tapping in some information. Anna began to worry. What if there were something wrong with her visa and she had to fly back home?

'Here to do some picking, eh?' the official asked.

'Yes, I am.'

'Have fun.'

And then she handed Anna her passport. Anna was through and officially now in Australia to start a new life. She couldn't be happier.

Her suitcase was already off-loaded from the carousel and standing with other luggage. She grabbed her bag and wheeled it to the exit and then down the ramp to the welcoming area and a sea of faces. Anna searched the faces before her. Where was Lucas, her hero's friend?

Through the crowd Anna spotted the young girl from her plane. She was also standing waiting. Could she be waiting for José's friend? And then a tap on Anna's shoulder.

'Hello, Anna?'

And there he was.

'I'm Lucas.'

And before he could continue: 'You're José's friend.' Anna leant up and kissed Lucas on both cheeks.

'Yes, I am José's friend and I'm very pleased to meet such a beautiful young girl. Welcome to Australia.'

Anna realised she had tears running down her face.

'I'm crying, I'm so happy. Forgive me.'

Lucas bent down to take Anna's luggage.

'I'm meeting another girl from Brazil and then I'll take you both for a clean-up and rest.'

And of course it was her. The girl from São Paulo. Anna knew it.

———

Both girls followed Lucas through the terminal and out to a car park. Lucas packed their luggage into the back of an SUV and told them to hop in. He handed each of the girls a bottle of water and a small muffin.

'We'll get real food into you at the house.'

And with that Lucas started the car and headed down the ramp and out into the dazzling Sydney sunshine.

Anna introduced herself to her new Brazilian companion.

'I'm Anna. I saw you in São Paulo. Are you a friend of José's too?'

'My name is Julianna. Very nice to meet you. Who is José?'

Anna explained to Julianna that it was through José's efforts that she was in Australia. Julianna then explained that it was through the efforts of Pedro that she was there. Pedro had befriended her and introduced her to the opportunities that lay ahead for her in Australia.

How similar our stories, thought Anna. And Lucas knew both José and Pedro. She must ask how later.

The sky was a Disney blue like you see in the movies. The SUV glided onto a freeway and within seconds it seemed began to cross a very large bridge shaped like a coat hanger.

'Sydney Harbour Bridge and Sydney Harbour below,' Lucas called out to the girls. 'Most beautiful harbour in the world.'

Anna and Julianna looked at each other and began giggling. This was going to be fun. Everything was new. Everything was interesting. Everything was cool. Especially the long tunnel the SUV purred through with the bright, blue-lit walls. And then out onto another freeway.

Anna wondered when the clean-up and rest would happen. They had been on the road for nearly two hours and she was in need of a pee. And then the SUV turned off the freeway onto a smaller road and ten minutes later onto a dirt road and then into the drive of what had to be a farm. Cattle and horses were in paddocks and dogs roamed the farmyard. There was no sign of fruit. The picking must be nearby somewhere.

Two men came from the farmhouse to meet the SUV as Lucas parked. He got out and joined them.

'A couple of little beauties, I must say,' one of the men smirked to Lucas.

'You know the Don's rules. Hands off the cargo,' said Lucas.

Anna looked to Julianna. A small dark cloud had descended on her wonderland.

'Alright, girls, into the house. Don't worry about your bags. We'll bring them.'

33

Adrian parked his ute a good distance from the bikie's house. Couple of k's from the gate. Could easily think it belonged to another farm. He didn't walk along the dirt road, instead hung behind the first line of trees. Kept him covered. There was a hiding place almost opposite the house. Bush covered in bougainvillea. And it was there he settled himself with his binoculars aimed at the house and waited. He still had the smile on his face thanks to Sheila. Strange, isn't it, how you think you know someone sorta well and then you get to know them sorta better. Same but different. Or something. Sheila was no pushover. Very able. Very able to cope with Mister Grumpy. Except Adrian hadn't been all that grumpy lately. Thoughts. More thoughts. Yep, thoughts that go round.

It was no later than nine and all was quiet at the house. Not a sign. Not a peep. Until there was. Ace and the third bikie came out and walked to the four-wheel, which looked to be loaded. Adrian picked up his camera, zeroing in on the tray. It was bulky with? With? What? Adrian moved the focus about. And then he saw. The tray was loaded with blankets. They looked like old army blankets. He snapped away as they began the drive down to the barn.

Adrian waited. Twenty minutes later the four-wheel was back, empty of blankets. They'd obviously been dumped at the barn. Meant to go with the mattresses. They were gearing up. Preparing for the fresh cargo. But when was the cargo due? That's what Adrian needed to know.

About two hours after dark Adrian decided to call it a night and head off. He would be back early the next morning.

———

The Don was feeling way on top of it. Lucas had phoned to say the cargo was on the move. An arrival from Sydney with more to come. Melbourne also had cargo on the road and would coordinate with the Sydney delivery. Not long to wait before the dollars rolled in. There was big money to be made. Big, big money. Might need to bash a few heads to guarantee it. Some outlets still needed to be nailed down. They were wavering. A little. But a little was too much, given the cargo was on its way. That was the Don's job and it was what made him happy. He'd risen in the ranks because no one said no to the Don. Some waverers had tried and they had reasons. Excellent reasons. Made out they had other allegiances. Scary allegiances. Heavy-duty you-could-die allegiances. But the Don sorted that. A disappearance or two usually resolved the impasse.

The Don was Serbian. Scary tough had been passed down to him from his father, a military man in the Bosnian conflict.

His father knew how to hate big time and ended up being convicted of war crimes. Only lasted a week in prison. Had his throat slashed. Taught the Don a lesson. Kill or be killed. The waverers would know about that come tomorrow.

The other two had been sent to set up the barn. Make it homely. The cargo would be kept there while it was in the process of being shipped to the outlets. They had mattresses and now blankets. That'd do. Didn't need to go overboard but did need them in good nick on delivery. There'll be whingers. Always are. But the barn might well be the best accommodation they'd get for the next two years or more. Should be grateful. They might see the barn as Buckingham Palace in later days.

On the boys' return and with confirmation that the barn was set up, the Don brought out the shotties and ammo.

'Clean and check 'em. Don't want any fuck-ups. Understand?'

The boys understood. They'd seen what happened when someone fucked up around the Don. There had been four of them once. A drug deal went bad and someone had to pay.

Whiskey with beer chasers was on the menu. That and conversation about the cargo. The fresh cargo requisitioned from South America. New cargo from a new source. Cheers.

———

Benny took in the handsome young man standing at the counter. He had introduced himself as Ryan, a friend of Leila's. He asked what time Leila would be on duty.

'She doesn't work here anymore, I'm afraid. Went a while back.'

'Know where she moved on to?'

'Sorry, no idea. Just bailed.'

Ryan was beyond disappointed and explained to Benny that they had been texting fairly regularly and that Leila had told him to come visit. That she loved working at The Basin. Weird that she hadn't mentioned she was moving on.

Benny offered the young man a coffee. Told him to take a seat. Ryan cut a sad figure sitting alone at the table. Benny was reminded of Sergeant Gallagher's inquiry a couple of days back concerning Leila's disappearance. Maybe the sarge knew more now. Benny brought a coffee to Ryan and had one for himself.

'If I drank with every customer I'd be flying, but happy to make an exception with you, Ryan.'

Ryan thanked Benny. He took a sip, then set about explaining his friendship with Leila and their meeting at Byron. How they seemed to be on the same wavelength about most stuff. He explained it was his background in medicine that led him to travel to Sydney to meet with Médecins Sans Frontières. They chatted for nearly an hour. Covered plenty of territory. Benny spoke of a terrible drowning along the beach. An Indigenous boy. A teenager. Sad. He talked of his Lebanese background while Ryan discussed his Iranian ancestry. Discussed the restrictions placed on each by their culture. The struggle that meant for each. Ryan was pleased to be able to talk with an older man about such restrictions. He could never talk with his father in that way.

Ryan thought he would hang around for a few days, find a chance to talk with the local cop. Benny pointed Ryan to the camping ground where there were cabins to rent. It was off-season so prices would be down. He mentioned to Ryan that there was always work available at The Basin if he was keen on earning a few bucks.

'Always a shift or two vacant.'

Ryan was keen. He decided he'd inquire at the camping ground immediately. He needed a bed for the night.

The cabin was clean and had a view of the beach. Surfers were out. Ryan wondered if the surfers knew how lucky they were. Of course they did. How could they not? He looked along the beach. Somewhere along there a boy had drowned. Life is so temporary, he thought. He needed to move forward with his life but first a swim and tomorrow a chat with Sergeant Gallagher.

———

As Ken paddled out, he noticed a young man walking along the beach. Could be Middle Eastern, something like that. Not Anglo, that was certain. The young man stopped and stripped down to a pair of bathers, and dived in. Ken hoped he knew what he was doing swimming in the ocean. Luckily it was a quiet day with easygoing waves. Hard to get into trouble today, Ken thought. They did, though. Out-of-towners. Never knew what a rip was and ended up screaming for help. Not today though and the young man seemed comfortable in the small waves.

Ken had romance on his mind. Conchita romance. They'd seen a lot of each other since the party. It was difficult to align times given she had her cafe to run. And she was diligent, so late evenings and early morning getaways were the answer. Love will find a way, they had decided. Ken hadn't had a relationship for several years. This was getting serious. For both of them. Conchita was good for him, he knew that. Softened him. Not that he was a particularly hard bastard, but he did pull back. Would go a little cold to protect himself. Didn't like getting too close. Holdover from childhood, of course. Wasn't everything? But Conchita was attending to the pullback by coming on. Clever woman, he thought.

There were a few clever women around. There was Wanda. Now, you didn't muck about with Wanda. And she was a writer. Ken had read several articles by her in the *Courier*. They were good. Smart. With humour. Ken wasn't sure humour could find a place in a story on David. So bloody terrible, the drowning. And yet only a few days before, Ken had chatted with the family in the park and the kid was saying no one needed to worry about him. Fuck. Life. It is random as.

Ken had checked with the family and they were cool with Wanda writing a piece. They also hoped it might help. They had a nag too. Didn't seem like something David would do. Go swimming at night in the ocean. He was a river rat. Something wasn't right. The family liked the idea. The sooner the better. And it was sooner with Wanda, as soon as Ken had told her she had the go-ahead.

Ken took off on a right-hander. It was nicely hollow. He grabbed the side of his board and let a little foam splash over his head. Straightened up and flicked off into a metre of water. So clear you could see the sand living down below. Moving to and fro. And that movement was what enabled Ken to see it. A phone on the seabed, dancing with the thousands of grains of sand that had kept it hidden. Well hidden.

Ken dived down and picked up the phone. He carried it and his board onto the beach. He laid his board down and sat on it. He held the phone in front of him. If only you could speak, he thought.

And then he thought: maybe you can.

34

Leila felt the room was becoming smaller. It wasn't, of course, she knew that. She wondered if prisoners felt that about their cells. If you let the mind take charge and whisper, 'It's getting smaller,' then you'd start to believe it. Leila knew every square millimetre of her cell, and it wasn't getting smaller.

He had changed since the murder of the boy. How long ago was that? Leila was having trouble with time. He was more on edge, more likely to fly off the handle. She had to be careful not to say the wrong thing. Whatever the wrong thing was. How was she to know with him?

He had started bashing her. Not crippling her but slapping her hard across the face if she upset him. That started when they returned to her room after the boy's death. It hurt. A lot. But Leila was a strong girl and wasn't giving into it by becoming hysterical. She steeled herself and then went quiet. Into herself. Cried when he left the room. And that's when it hit her. She had witnessed a murder. She had watched a boy being drowned. There was nothing she could do to stop it. Did that make her a party to the death? Surely you are meant to stop such atrocities, but she did nothing. There it was again, the mind trying to fuck her up. Staying in the present was the answer to getting through this. Easier said than done. You bet. She'd seen him kill the boy and he knew it. Would he let her live with that knowledge?

His behaviour was erratic. That was the word. His visits were now not only morning and night but at odd times during the day. Or not at all. He'd finished the job he'd been on. A barn somewhere. And didn't he love telling her how skilled he was. Leila made sure she enthused about his ability. That made him happy and want to lie down with her and wrap his arms around her or have her cuddle him. It was revolting, but Leila wanted to live. And then there would be the times when he didn't believe her and a bashing would follow.

They would still go for their drives in his car. His pride and joy that never left the shed. He would tell Leila that he'd washed and polished the car so it would look beautiful for her. Leila would thank him. They drove across the country one week. Five days in a row they sat in the car with their eyes closed talking about the scenery.

It was hard. Fucking hard not to go insane. There was the real Leila kidnapped and kept in a fucking dungeon desperately trying to survive. And then there was the fantasy Leila cuddling a madman and going on make-believe drives.

Leila was not going to give in. Leila would be alive and sane when they found her. Whoever they were. Whenever that was.

35

Sergeant Gallagher drove to the beach as soon as Ken rang. The phone. It had to be David's. Please. The pair of them walked the beach on the off-chance there was something else. Something of David's. Like his clothes. But no luck. Only the phone. The sarge would bag it and have it sent straight to Sydney. Hopefully there was something on it that would help.

Ken wasn't sure what he'd seen after his moonlight surf on the night of the drowning. He told the sarge there was someone down at the three-kilometre mark. Must have been near 9 pm. No, he couldn't make out who or what was going on but someone was there, where David's body was found the next morning. The sergeant asked Ken if he was aware of a white van around that time near the beach. Ken couldn't help the sarge.

The sarge thought maybe the article Wanda was writing might elicit some info. He was all for the article, as long as it wasn't sensationalist. Wanda had assured him it wouldn't be. She'd asked the sarge if he'd prefer to be there when she spoke with Moira and the family but he didn't think it necessary. Ken had cleared it with Moira. That's all that mattered. He was grateful that both Wanda and Ken had felt it necessary to talk with him first. Not that they needed police permission. The sarge began to believe that his nag might be on the way out. He bloody hoped so.

The sarge and Ken walked back along the beach. The afternoon was turning into evening. The young man Ken had spotted earlier was standing by the sarge's police car.

'Excuse me, officer, my name is Ryan and I am a friend of Leila Sodahl. I'm worried about her disappearance. Could I please talk to you about her?'

'Not right now you can't, mate, I'm a little busy, but why don't you come by the police station tomorrow?'

'Thank you, sir, thank you. Tomorrow morning.'

And then Ryan turned and set off for his cabin. Ken and the sarge watched him leave.

'Some movement suddenly.'

'Seems like it, Sarge. Hope it leads to something positive.'

'You never know, Ken. You never know.'

The sarge got into his car and headed back to the station.

Ken strapped his board onto his racks. Took a last look at the surf and started up. He sat for a moment. Interesting arvo, he thought. And now, home or Conchita?

Not even a question. It had to be Conchita. Ken was falling big time and he didn't mind. Not at all. He sent her a text.

'Be kissing your neck in twenty.'

Then straight into gear and off with a smile.

36

Both Anna and Julianna had made good use of the bathroom at the farmhouse. They had been busting. It was another twenty minutes before Lucas and one of the other men joined them inside. They had the girls' bags. The girls were seated on an old lounge waiting. Lucas explained that they would stay here at the farmhouse until another group of girls arrived.

'It should only be a day or two.'

'And then where do we move to and when do we start the fruit picking?'

At this the other man began to laugh. Anna found this strange. Why would he laugh? she thought.

'Why are you laughing?'

Lucas waved the man away.

'He's laughing because he's an idiot. Take no notice of him. Your fruit picking is being sorted right now. Don't you worry.'

Anna wasn't worried, but she decided she did not enjoy the idiot.

Lucas showed the girls to a room with four bunk beds in it. He explained they would sleep here until they moved on and then he left them. The girls each chose a bed and began to unpack.

'I don't have my passport or my phone in my bag, Anna,' said Julianna.

Anna searched her bag. Both her phone and passport were also missing.

Julianna began to cry.

'What have we got ourselves into, Anna?'

Anna lowered herself to sit on the bed. She couldn't answer Julianna's question.

———

'We want our passports and phones returned, Lucas. You have no right to take them.'

Anna had dealt with stupid men who tried to control her and she'd stood up to them and she would do the same with Lucas.

Lucas explained that the girls had a very large debt that they needed to pay off. That his company had done everything to help them but they were not a charity. Flying such a distance on so many airlines and securing visas was an expensive business.

'You will work to pay off this debt and then you will be given back your phones and passports. It's our guarantee you'll not run off. Everything will be fine. You wait and see.'

Anna wasn't happy.

'Then hurry up and get us to work, please.'

The idiot smiled at Anna.

'Don't worry, you'll be working very soon.'

———

After dinner that night—if you could call lukewarm canned beans on a piece of stale bread a dinner—Anna and Julianna made a pact that they would look out for each other no matter what happened. They came up with a plan not to antagonise Lucas and the other men. They would be courteous and obliging and grateful, but always cautious and ready. Ready for what, they had no idea. They were here to work, and the sooner that started the better. Once they were working, everything would be wonderful. Like they had imagined. Neither girl slept particularly well that night.

Anna woke early. She dressed and went out onto the back veranda. The idiot was sitting there smoking. Anna said hello, asked him how he was, commented on the nice day ahead and then went back inside. She found a glass and filled it with water from the tap over the sink. Drank it down. Then she went out onto the front veranda. The third man was there, sitting back on a chair and smoking. She greeted him cheerfully, commented on the day ahead, received a grunt in reply, and then retreated once again back into the house.

In her room Anna thought about waking Julianna. She sat on her bed looking at a young girl so like herself. Someone searching for more out of life than was available in Brazil. She let her sleep. There was no point in worrying Julianna any further. Anna didn't like both front and back verandas being guarded. That was her conclusion but was she being paranoid? She had woken early. Couldn't they have? Maybe they were being thoughtful by not smoking in the house.

Who was she kidding? They were definitely making sure the girls didn't run off. To where? Anna wondered. She had no idea where they were. North or south, she couldn't tell. Not a clue. She had to stop the worrying. It wouldn't help.

Anna decided a coffee might help and went back to the kitchen. Lucas was there and a pot of coffee was brewing.

'Hi, like a cup?' he said.

Anna replied that she would love one.

'And how about Julianna?'

Anna thought yes, Julianna would enjoy a cup as well.

Lucas poured two cups and handed them to Anna.

'Enjoy.'

Anna thanked Lucas and returned to the bedroom with the coffees. Maybe everything would be okay, she thought.

37

Benny drove Ryan to the police station. Ryan told the sarge that he believed something bad had happened to Leila Sodahl. The sarge listened. That was one of the things he'd learnt from the top cops he'd watched during his time. They listened even when it was waffle and barmy ideas. Why, he'd asked one top cop. Why listen to so much bullshit? And the top cop told him that sometimes, just sometimes, there's a gold nugget in with the bullshit.

'Gold nuggets are our lifeblood, mate. Can't solve fuck-all without a gold nugget or two.'

Ryan didn't have any gold nuggets to explain his fear for the girl's safety. He did have a genuine affection for her, and the sarge could see that. And Ryan wasn't a fuckwit. The sarge felt Ryan had a decent understanding of the girl's behaviour. And there were two problems with her behaviour. Just pissing off from The Basin without so much as a 'see you later, alligator' was one, and the other was not staying in contact as she had been doing. Still, people aren't always consistent, the sarge knew that. Often an occasion arises that bends us into a different shape for a while. It was the occasion that troubled the sarge. Harmless or criminal?

The sarge thanked Ryan for his help. Said the file was remaining open on Leila's disappearance and to let him know if he heard from her.

———

Ryan felt good. He was grateful to Benny for giving him a lift. Following things through was important. He'd seen how important in his short time helping out at Médecins Sans Frontières. They dotted their i's and crossed their t's. No mucking about there. Ryan had decided to stay on. He liked the cabin by the beach and had negotiated a good deal for his stay. His negotiating skills had been honed selling drugs in his younger days. Nothing is ever wasted, it seemed to Ryan. He smiled at the thought.

'So, okay if I do a few shifts? I'm staying on while the sarge keeps the investigation open.'

Benny was only too happy to agree. He liked having Ryan around. Ryan reminded Benny of a younger Benny. A vulnerable Benny. A brave Benny. It was being brave that scared him now.

The sarge had talked to all of them after the drowning. Did they see anything? Remember anything?

Why didn't Benny speak up? Why didn't he say he had a delivery around that time on the night in question. For a bloody good reason, that's why. The delivery had been fucking weed. Great help that would have been. In fucking up his life. Rationalising didn't help. Of course it had nothing to do with the drowning, but he should have spoken up. Maybe the fella saw something. Who knows? Benny ripped the thoughts out of his brain. How long would that last?

When he dropped Ryan back at the camping ground he asked if he was okay for a shift at lunchtime.

'You bet. See you in an hour and thanks. Talking to the sarge made me feel better.'

Benny sat in the car. The thoughts came back. He knew what he had to do.

38

Adrian had been in hiding near the bikie's house since 6 am. Just light when he woke, got up and made a coffee. The wind was offshore and if the swell hadn't changed overnight a wave was to be had. But not by him. Not this morning. Not until this was over.

He was glad he'd been sharp in getting to his hidey-hole, because movement was happening at the house. Lights were on. An hour later the four-wheel rolled down the drive and out the gate. The four-wheel stopped so the gate could be secured again and then sped off with the three bikies on board.

This was a tricky one. Adrian raced through the bush to his ute. He nearly killed himself jumping in and starting the thing and taking off all in one movement. Did a doughnut backing out onto the track and then gunned it. The four-wheel had a big fucking start but there really was only one place it could head to. The freeway entrance. But which way then? North or south? Adrian had to be able to clock the direction it took. And he did. North.

The drive was no longer than twenty minutes. Adrian knew the town they drove into. He'd surfed there. Not a bad spot. Had a cinema. Had a cool restaurant-bar that shook on the weekends. He'd shaken there with an attractive one-nighter one night. The attractive one-nighter probably remembers shaking there with a one-nighter herself.

On the outskirts the four-wheel parked out front of a large two-storey timber house with a glowing red light hanging over the doorway. Massage parlour upstairs, living quarters downstairs. Adrian pulled in fifty metres further on at the next corner. He watched as the Don and Ace went to the door. They knocked. Barged in as it was opened. The third bikie stayed in the four-wheel. Adrian thought about slipping past. Maybe get a geek through a window. But there wasn't much chance of that. Thought about pretending to be a client, but that was about as stupid as it gets, given they knew him. Too much of a coincidence. Way too much.

At the back of the house there was a vacant block facing onto the street behind. Adrian grabbed his camera. Sprinted around the corner and onto the vacant block. Carefully hoisted himself over the wooden fence. Now he was at the back of the house. Nothing at the first window. On to the next. A small opening in the curtain and there they were. The Don had a shottie aimed at the head of an Asian boy no older than ten. He was gripping the boy's hair to keep him still. Adrian snapped a couple. The boy looked terrified, as did the man and woman with him. Had to be the boy's mother and father. Adrian watched. He could see the father pleading and then falling to his knees and nodding. Nodding. And nodding more.

Finally the Don took the shottie from the boy's head and leant down to pull the father up off his knees. Smiled, then put his hand out to the father, who took it and shook it. The Don followed up putting his arm around the father, who was weeping. All was good now. The Don had got what he wanted.

———

Next the four-wheel journeyed to a building by the airport. Street or two back. Again a red light signalling what lay inside. Flesh. Same story. The Don and Ace barged through the door.

There was no way Adrian would get a look in here, but he imagined the scene inside.

Coercion. Shotgun to the head. An ultimatum. Adrian had his phone ready in case the coercion didn't work and a shottie exploded, delivering death to a waverer. But it worked. It always worked when it was the Don delivering the ultimatum. And again there'd be a nodding inside the house, acknowledging that a new supplier would be delivering the flesh from now on.

Two hours later and a further two visits. No shotgun blasts. Deal done tight. Very professional.

39

Benny had left a message for Adrian. It was an urgent message. He needed to talk out his problem. Benny trusted Adrian. Phew. How good is that thought? He trusted a bloke who helped Benny set up a drug dealership. It wasn't a drug dealership, for fuck's sake. It was selling a little weed to friends. He was helping out. It was a helping-out dealership. Benny's mind was running round in circles.

The sooner they legalised weed the better. Benny had always thought that. Must cost a bomb tracking it down and it would rid the game of the big crims. The scary crims. The nasty crims. The ones with the drug dealerships who treated everyone like scum.

Benny never treated anyone like scum. Benny loved everyone. He sure loved his staff. Staff were precious. He was keen to see how Ryan would go on the lunchtime shift. It was working. On the ball. Charmed the customers. Perfecto. Thank the lucky stars. It wasn't easy getting staff. Any staff, let alone good staff. And Ryan was good. Benny hoped he'd stick around for a bit. Make up for losing Leila.

Benny closed up and decided a late surf would be the answer to his angst. And it was. Ken was out already so the two of them shared the best of what was on offer. Sweet metre-high waves. As Benny finished and was drying off, Adrian arrived. He'd seen Benny's message, checked Benny's home and The Basin and then figured he had to be down the beach.

'You messaged me?'

'Yep, I did. Can we talk back at my place? It's private and Ken will be out in a moment, and—well, if we could go to my house, that would be better.'

'Sure.'

'Thanks.'

And the pair of them set out for Benny's house with Benny carrying his nine-foot epoxy surfboard and Adrian wondering what could be on Benny's mind.

————

Benny poured them both a beer. They sat on his veranda as the sun was going down. Beautiful. A pink-sky evening.

'Spill it, then. What's the go?'

And so Benny spilt it. Rambled a bit about how stupid he was in the first place to get involved in dealing drugs. Adrian let him ramble. Rambled further about not owning up to the sarge. Should have spoken up, et cetera, et cetera, et cetera.

'Owned up to what, Benny?'

Benny told him. Told Adrian how he'd had a delivery that night after nine from their supplier. The night David drowned.

'You mean your supplier, Benny. You're selling the weed, not me.'

'Yeah, but you get a free bag.'

'Lucky me. But you're selling it, Benny.'

Benny slumped forward, face in hands.

'Yep. You're right. But that shouldn't have stopped me. I should have spoken up. I mean, the fella might have seen something. Something important that could've helped the sarge.'

'Doubt it, Benny.'

And then Adrian calmed Benny telling him the boy drowned. Nothing to do with Benny. Not to be hard on himself.

Told Benny it was their little secret. The weed.

'Don't sweat it, mate. Okay?'

'Yeah, okay, Adrian, if you think that's the way to go. Thanks. Thanks for coming over. Thanks for putting me right. I was letting it get to me.'

'Nice evening.'

'Yeah, nice evening, Adrian. Ta, mate.'

They sat finishing their beers, watching pink turn to black. It was a nice evening for them sitting out on Benny's veranda. Both with plenty going on in their heads.

40

The *Courier* with Wanda's article on David was lying on Wanda's dining room table. The morning light gave it a halo. She picked it up. She needed another ego hit. A two-page spread with photographs of the family—Moira, Wayne and Marcia, but not of David. That wasn't culturally permissible. However, they had given permission for David's name to be used. Wanda had given it her all and the result made her feel proud. She loved writing but not a lot of room for it up the coast. Maybe this would stir action from down Sydney way. You never knew where or when the light would shine. Didn't matter, she knew she'd done a great job. Wayne had already been in touch to say the family were happy. There was a great photo of David's room with all his posters, and in the centre his pride and joy, the GTS Monaro poster.

Wanda had focused the article on the spirit of the Indigenous kids. She decided she wasn't an academic, she'd leave colonisation and history to others. Kids were more important. Their love of life and love of adventure. She wrote about the restrictions on kids playing in places these days. On how playgrounds were all wrapped in cotton wool. She wrote about how the Indigenous kids went for it. If they broke something, so what? How else do you learn? Living is learning. She got on a roll and got a little off-track in talking about adults and their self-help books, feeling they needed to understand life from reading rather than experiencing. It wasn't that hard to understand. It was in front of you. Go for it, you can only fail. And failure is part of the journey to success. There are no guarantees. Just today. And that's what we could all learn from the spirit of young David. She had to bring it back. She knew she'd got carried away. Anyway, she felt good. Real bloody good.

Wanda wrote that David's death was still under investigation and that if anyone had any knowledge of David's last few hours it would be immensely helpful to the police.

Wanda sat staring at the *Courier* in her hands. She carefully folded the paper and placed it back on the dining table and went to the fridge, took out her full cream milk, and made a cuppa. She took it out onto the veranda and settling in to her good old falling-apart outside chair, she smiled as she read her article once again.

———

They had arranged an early morning meeting at the airport. First flight in from Sydney was at five past seven. Adrian was in the cafe waiting. He had his camera with him. The supervisor settled himself and asked for an update. Adrian filled him in, then showed him the shots he'd taken yesterday.

'Lucky that bloke gave in. Cunt would have shot the kid. No qualms. Nothing scares those bastards. There's no authority but them.'

The word from the inside was that all the girls had arrived and were now in various stages of being transported up the coast. The feds were on alert and ready to go when called. Adrian was to stand by. Keep watch.

Adrian confirmed he was on top of it. Had a nice stake-out position and would know when the girls were settled at the farm.

'Yeah, okay. We'll talk.'

'Just one thing.'

'What's that?'

Adrian wanted to discuss the drowning of an Indigenous boy before he shot off. There was some heat building with it and the local sergeant wasn't sure if it was an accident. He was asking around.

'What's that to do with us?'

Adrian told him that Benny was thinking he should tell the sarge he had a visitor on the night of the drowning, around the time a van was seen in the area. A van the sarge was interested in. Adrian was sure it had nothing to do with the kid's death, but the visitor was the fella that got him the job fixing the bikies' barn. The fella Adrian had put Benny in contact with for drugs. And he had a van. It was becoming messy.

The supervisor knew of the drowning. Word had come through that the kid's phone had been found.

'Pretty fucked over being in the ocean that long. Nothing helpful. Head office see it as a drowning.'

'Nothing to see on the phone?'

'Nope. Last photo was blurry. An old car. No use. Is Benny going to see the sarge?'

'No, I talked him out of it. For the moment.'

The bloke told Adrian to keep it like that until the bikie bust was done.

'We don't want the local cops to fuck our operation. After we're done they can go for it.'

The two men shook hands.

'Soon.'

'Yep. Soon.'

And then they went their separate ways.

Adrian sat for a while in his ute. Things were hotting up. A bust was imminent. It was a big deal. It could blow a massive hole in the organised crime syndicate dealing in sex trafficking of young girls in New South Wales. Adrian liked that idea. He turned on the ignition, slipped into gear and moved out of the airport car park.

———

It was a little before nine when Adrian set his binoculars on the farmhouse. Quiet as a mouse if a farmhouse can be a mouse. Bloody stupid saying. Adrian smiled. Can't be that quiet. Cats seem to hear mice pretty damn well.

Adrian noticed he was feeling anxious. If they pulled off this bust it could mean he'd be asked to scope another territory. He didn't want another territory. He was liking it here. The surf, the coffee, and now Sheila and the discount on cleaning that went with Sheila. Smiling again. They'd sent him up here because info had leaked that big stuff might be happening. That was the talk. Plans being devised. Adrian was keen when they offered the posting. He'd really needed to get away. But now he was calling this place home. Could he leave and set up again? Probably. There would be another Sheila in another place.

It wasn't easy living a lie. How do those spooks do it? Adrian couldn't imagine himself spying in Russia or China. If you were found out they didn't kill you, you were locked away forever. No one ever heard of you again. With under-cover, if you were found out it was all over. A bullet in the head. Done. Gone.

Not much movement at the farmhouse. Adrian settled in. He'd picked up the local *Courier* at the airport. Thought he may as well take a glance at what extraordinary goings-on were happening. Look up the tides. Check the weather. See how the fishing was. Not a lot happened on his part of the coast. Was he crazy? Here he was preparing for a major bust, not to mention the small drug operation he had set up. Smiling again.

Wanda's article on the kid's drowning took up a middle spread in the paper. Adrian heard Wanda wrote the odd article. Not that he'd read any. Too busy noticing what a good sort she was.

The article was impressive. She knew what she was doing. Adrian wondered if you needed to go to university to become a journalist. The article was very positive about the Indigenous community. He liked that. The funeral was a turning point for Adrian. It gave him a better understand-ing of the importance of family to them. He thought Anglos needed to get their house in order regarding family before they went off at the Indigenous.

Adrian remembered the temptations around when he was growing up. The pressures to fit in as a young bloke. But now social media and drugs and booze and gambling. Bigger pressures for sure.

He enjoyed the article and reminded himself to congratulate Wanda next time he saw her. He liked the photo of the poster of the GTS Monaro. Popular bloody car. Old car.

Holy shit, old car.

Adrian made a call.

———

It was around midday when the three SUVs pulled in at the farmhouse. Lucas met them at the gate. Unlocked it. Let them through. Relocking it after. Three SUVs and seven girls.

The idiot came down from the veranda licking his lips.

Same story. The girls were told to leave their bags and guided to the bathroom. There was a separate loo in the laundry for some to use. Then they were taken into the rooms for their night stay.

Anna and Julianna watched from their bedroom window. Their door was opened and two of the girls ushered in. The idiot was with them.

'These two are sharing with you tonight.'

And then he left with a parting slimy leer. Anna and Julianna introduced themselves, asking where in South America the girls were from.

'My name is Antonia and this is Francesca.'

Both were from Argentina, and both had been enticed by the promises of big money to be made in Australia. They had arrived as had the other girls only that morning.

The door opened again, and the idiot deposited the girls' bags into the room. He spoke to Anna and Julianna.

'Need you girls out here to rustle up sandwiches. Everyone's hungry. You've got five minutes.'

Anna shut the door behind the idiot.

'Please check your bags for your passports and phones.'

The girls did, emptying the contents onto the beds. No passports. No phones.

Anna explained to the new girls the reason they were given, for their phones and passports being held by Lucas.

'Hopefully it will be okay, but we must look out for each other I think.'

The girls agreed.

Anna and Julianna hugged each of the girls.

'We will be alright together, I am sure.'

41

Ken had stayed the night at Conchita's. He'd gone there after his late afternoon surf. It was a fun surf, with Benny joining him for an hour or so. He liked Benny. Liked how Benny had made something of The Basin. It was a real community hangout. This was a real worry thinking like this. Thinking community. What's next? It was strange but since David's drowning he was starting to appreciate where he was and what he had here on the coast. Conchita. He totally appreciated what his job had given him. That was real. Sense of purpose and a use of his qualifications. But normal everyday stuff he'd been taking for granted.

He had watched Benny wandering off with Adrian, chatting away after his surf. Ken didn't realise they were that close and wondered what it was they were discussing. Maybe he was noticing the interaction between the locals. Hadn't really done that before. Noticed. Bit self-absorbed could that be the reason? Was Conchita opening his eyes to others? Can't be bad, he thought. Good for Conchita. Good for me.

And then there was the conversation with Brian as he was strapping his board on. Brian had driven up asked him if he had a moment. All sorts of strange things happening. Brian had never asked him if he had a moment. Never. But he did here. Brian told Ken he had a problem that he'd like to talk over with Ken. The new Ken. So the less self-absorbed Ken said, 'Sure, Brian. How can I help you?'

And Brian told Ken about seeing a van the night of David's drowning and that he'd told the sarge but that he didn't see the van properly or who was driving because the headlights were in his eyes.

'Yeah. And?'

And then Brian continued with his story of the van and said that a day or so ago he'd waved to a bloke driving a van. The bloke driving the van was someone he'd sold a small farm to a few months back.

'And?'

And then Brian asked whether, since Ken was a lawyer, he thought he should mention this to the sarge.

Ken finished strapping his board on. Thought about the question.

'Lotta blokes have vans, Brian. I think unless you really feel it may be the van the sarge was interested in then I'd leave it. The sarge has a lot on his plate.'

Brian thanked Ken for his advice.

'That's helpful. Yep, helpful. Thanks, Ken.'

And then Brian was off.

Brian was a little on edge. A little. Are you joking? Brian was all over the shop. The fact that the sarge knew he'd been playing tootsies and more with Wanda filled him with dread, even though Wanda assured him the sarge wasn't about to spill all to Nolene. And then Nolene had been in Melbourne for three days with not so much as a text to say she missed him. Probably didn't. Why would she miss a deceitful fucking two-timing prick like Brian?

Life was getting far too complicated. Once he had a lovely loyal wife and he was a loyal husband and he sold real estate and he was good at it. It was easy. Sign here, money in the bank.

He'd ring Nolene, that was the answer. Ring her and make her laugh and she would miss him and come racing back and he'd never go near Wanda or any woman that wasn't his wife ever again. God's truth. God wasn't going to have anything to do with him. So onto the phone and no answer. Leave a message.

'Hi, darling. It's me. Missing you. Call me. Kisses.'

Where was she? Was she onto him? Couldn't be. Fuck, life is complicated.

And that's when he decided to uncomplicate some of it and go talk to Ken. And that's what he did and it uncomplicated some of it. Didn't it? Yeah, of course it did. Didn't it?

42

He opened the wooden door and then the grille door. He carried a suitcase and was smiling.

'Surprise. You will love this.'

And the fella opened the suitcase and brought out a long white dress.

'My mother's wedding dress. Beautiful, isn't it?'

And then he displayed the dress in all its beauty by holding it with his arms stretched outward.

'Well?'

Leila knew she had to answer, but what to say? If her whole time locked in the room wasn't terrifying enough, this was more than she could cope with.

Leila began to weep.

'Why are you crying?'

Leila wiped her eyes.

'Because it is so beautiful. She must have looked very beautiful wearing it on her wedding day.'

The fella stared at Leila. Leila was terrified. Would he bash her?

'Put it on. Put the wedding dress on.'

And the fella held the wedding dress out to Leila.

Leila was at a loss. He was mad. That was the only answer. Mad. Mad. Mad.

'Put it on now.'

'But it's your mother's wedding dress. I don't deserve to wear your mother's wedding dress.'

'Yes, you do, that's why I've brought it down here. Put it on.'

Leila could feel her heart pounding. Her body trembling.

'Look, why don't you leave it with me for a while? Give me a chance to clean up. Fix my hair a little. This is a dress I need to honour. Don't you think?'

Leila waited. The fella began to nod.

'Yes, it does need to be honoured. I'll come back. You will be beautiful like my mother.'

Leila took the dress.

The fella turned back through the doors, locking them behind him.

———

Leila stood frozen. She wasn't sure for how long. She knew now he would never set her free from the room.

Leila folded the dress and laid it on the bed. How long did she have before he came back? An hour? A day?

She splashed water on her hands and wiped her face. She had no idea if her face was clean or filthy. She began to comb her hair with her fingers. Her fingernails had grown and that helped.

She undressed.

She took the dress and pulled it over her head. She fixed the fasteners. Leila vowed she would not die in the wedding dress.

43

The evening was coming on. Anna and Julianna had made sandwiches for the girls and the men. There were now seven men. The girls were told that they would be on the move early the next morning.

'Where to?' Anna asked Lucas.

'On your way to the fruit picking. Sound good?'

It did sound good. Very good. The girls were delighted and relieved. Then it was back to their rooms.

Anna was sitting on her bed talking with Francesca when the idiot came into the room.

'You two follow me.' And he pointed to Julianna and Antonia.

The girls looked to Anna, then rose and followed the idiot. The door to their bedroom was closed after them.

'Where do you think they have gone?' Francesca asked Anna.

Anna shook her head. She had no idea.

———

The girls were taken across the yard to a small cabin holding four beds, obviously where the men slept while taking turns guarding the girls.

In the room were Lucas and one of the drivers. The idiot ushered the girls in, then exited, closing the door behind him.

Lucas and the driver had been drinking. There were glasses and bottles on a table.

'Got drinks for you girls. Party time. Be glad to get out of that room, eh?'

Both Julianna and Antonia refused drinks.

'Why are we here?' Julianna asked.

'Why are you here? Why are you here? To have a good time, of course. South American girls love to party, I've been told.'

And then Lucas put on music from his phone.

'Let's see you dance.'

The girls stood frozen to the spot. Terrified.

'I said, let's see you dance.'

The girls didn't move.

'So no dancing, is it?'

The girls said nothing. Lucas and the driver smiled at each other.

'I guess it's time for some fruit picking then, isn't it?'

And Lucas and the driver grabbed a girl each and slammed her onto a bed.

———

The idiot was standing outside the door listening. He was furious he hadn't been invited to the party. But he knew there would be other parties at other times. This game was going to go on for a long time, with a lot more South American beauties here to pick fruit.

He smiled as he heard screams. The girls were being told how to behave. He could hear the slaps. Heavy slaps. The idiot enjoyed listening to the fun being played out behind the door.

————

When the door eventually opened and the girls came out, even the idiot was taken aback at the state of the two girls. They were pale and trembling with bruises and cuts on their faces. They carried some of their clothing. Not all had been ripped from their bodies. They were in shock, unable to comprehend the violation they had experienced. The idiot led the weeping girls back to the farmhouse and into the bedroom. He shut the bedroom door.

The girls went straight to their beds and sobbed into them. Anna and Francesca quietly hugged each girl. There was no talking. There was no need for talking. They now knew what the fruit-picking job they had signed up for entailed. They were to be the fruit. They would be sold off to men for sex.

44

Adrian was back in his hole. Had been there since before dawn. He had waited until sun-up to speak to his supervisor, who confirmed that the cargo would be arriving in the next few hours and that a bust would be on soon afterwards. He would be given a call when he should make himself scarce. That was the problem with doing undercover. You often missed out on the fun. Not always. But yeah, no point in being undercover only to be uncovered.

Adrian couldn't help but wonder who was providing the info. Who was the informer? Had to be someone on the inside. Up here or down there? Adrian knew he'd never know.

What he did know, however, was that the big old car on David's phone was a Monaro. His supervisor told him that.

Adrian had made the call after reading Wanda's article and seeing a picture of David's favourite poster. Was it possible? Probably not. A coincidence? No such thing. A Monaro. Bloody hell. And Adrian was stuck here in his hole until told to fuck off.

Adrian waited. Watched. Had the binoculars up and down. Nothing going on. Sweet fuck-all. And then sweet fuck-all became sweet fuck-everything. Three SUVs at the gate. Almost midday. The first two had a driver and three girls. The third also had a goon in the back keeping an eye on the operation.

———

It had been a long drive. A long silent drive. Some of the girls slept or tried to sleep, but not Anna. From the moment they left their farmhouse prison, Anna had taken note of her surroundings. She noted the sun had risen on her right so knew she was travelling north. The car radio showed the time of leaving to be 7.11 am. She had impressed on her mind the twists and turns taken to reach the freeway from the farmhouse. And now she had arrived at another farmhouse. The time was 11.26 am. A journey of four hours. To what?

The gate was locked. Within minutes two men came down to open the gate and wave the SUVs through. Large dogs trotted behind them. Each of the men climbed into one of the first two vehicles and spoke to the drivers. The SUVs then proceeded to follow a track past a farmhouse and on to a barn, where they pulled in. The men hopped out. One spoke. It was Ace.

'Out we get, girls. It's home sweet home. Hope the drive was enjoyable.'

The barn doors were opened.

'We call this Buckingham Palace and we know you girls will love it.'

The open doors revealed a large space covered in mattresses with blankets and pillows thrown haphazardly about.

'In we go, ladies.'

The girls looked at each other before slowly entering the barn.

'There are toilets up the front of Buck House and a table with water for washing. Some grub will be brought down in a little while, so make yourselves at home. Oh, and don't think about running off, the doggies don't like that.'

And then the men proceeded to dump the girls' bags in the barn. The barn doors were slammed shut. Anna heard a padlock being fitted.

———

Ace reported to the Don that all was as it should be. Nine girls. Nine pretty girls with two bearing a little bruising. The Don nodded.

'Guess they needed some understanding knocked into them. Boys must have been sampling the cargo.'

'When do we get to sample?' asked Ace.

The Don smiled.

'When I say so. Right now, it's time to report the cargo has arrived.' The Don made a call.

It was decided two of the SUVs would remain. The third would return south with the three drivers and their goon buddy after food and drinks. The Don nominated the return driver. He would stay sober.

'No fucking way. Why me?'

'Because I said.'

The Don then ordered the third bikie to head off in the ute and find lunch. Girls needed to be fed.

'Have to look healthy on delivery, don't they? And we need more grog.'

The bikie was given a roll of notes while beers were passed round.

———

Adrian had the binoculars out. He'd scribbled down the numberplates and occupants. Nine women and four men, and then Ace and his mate had wandered down to open the gate. He called. Passed on the information and was told to wait and watch. Which is what he did. Waited and watched. Watched the ute motor down the drive and head towards town. Made another call.

'Should I follow?'

And was told definitely not.

'Get ready to move when I tell you.'

———

Anna took Julianna by the arm and led her to a mattress.

'You lie here. Rest.'

The other girls grabbed their belongings and chose mattresses. Anna then asked Francesca to lift her to the shutters. Anna struggled to see out.

'What do you see?'

'The men have gone but the dogs are there.'

Anna slid down. All the girls looked to her. Why were they looking to her? And then it came to her.

Non ducor, duco.

I am not led, I lead.

No, Anna thought. Not here. She was in the same night-mare as all the girls. She had no way out. She couldn't lead. Couldn't possibly. She was Anna who worked at reception at the car hire firm in São Carlos in Brazil. She was being held captive by very bad men on the other side of the world. How could she lead anything?

'We should get some rest. That is the best thing for us to do right now. There will be food soon.'

Anna looked to Julianna, who smiled at her as the girls settled down on the mattresses.

45

The drink was getting low. Bloody low. The Don had the shits. Not good when the Don has the shits.

'Where's that food and extra grog? Fucker's taking his time. Ace, go get a couple of the girls. Let's have some fun. Get the two who know the score. Won't be any argument there, I reckon.'

Ace went to the door. But then the Don changed his mind.

'No, I'll get them myself.'

And taking a beer and his shottie, the Don headed for the barn.

Inside the barn, Anna and the girls could hear the dogs barking and then there was the sound of the padlock being opened. The Don appeared, pulling the door shut behind him.

'Hi, ladies, how we going? Enjoying the barn?'

No one spoke.

'Me and the boys have a little party going up at the house and we're inviting you two girls who partied so well earlier. You have great recommendations. So come on, girls, let's go.'

No one moved. The Don lifted his shottie.

'Let's not fuck around now, girls. Front and centre. Now.'

Not a movement.

'Now, fuck it. Now.'

Anna moved forward.

'Sir, I like to party. Very much. Please may I come?'

'That's better. Much better. And what's your name, little sister?'

'I'm Anna. I party very much. You will like, I am sure, sir.'

And Anna shone in front of the Don. Sexy as. The Don was transfixed.

'You come over here, my lovely. You get to party with the Don.'

Anna walked over to beside the Don. He placed his arm around her waist, lowering the shottie in his other hand. He moved forward.

'So who's joining Anna here to party?'

The Don smiled at the girls standing in front of him.

And then it happened. So fast. Anna smashed her fist up into the Don's face. Julianna threw herself at him, clawing and screaming. And then the other seven girls dragged him to the ground. The Don lost control of the shottie. He tried to scramble to his feet. No chance. The nine were all over him. Punching. Clawing. Biting. It was savage. It was anger. The Don got what he wanted. He was fucked. And they didn't let up until Anna called a halt.

'Who can use this?'

Anna held up the shottie. Julianna stepped forward to take it.

'My father hunts. We have many guns.'

———

The Don had been gone for over twenty minutes. Inside the house the men were getting fidgety.

'What's he doin'? Not sharin', it looks like to me.'

And Ace walked to the door. There was no sign of the Don.

'Right, I'm going down. He's not havin' it all. When the grog and food arrive, yell out.'

And Ace set off for the barn.

———

The call came through to Adrian. He was to vamoose. The bust was on. Five heavy-duty cop cars were on the road. Adrian grabbed his backpack and binoculars and headed to his ute, parked out front of the neighbouring farm.

———

The dogs began barking as Ace approached the barn. He pulled the door open and entered. Lying on the concrete floor in front of him was mangled flesh. Still breathing mangled flesh. Just. The flesh was leaking blood. An eye was out of its socket. There didn't seem to be a nose on the face. Not a pretty sight.

Ace raised his shottie and as he did the girls parted to reveal Julianna with the Don's shottie aimed fair at Ace's chest. And that was what exploded just after Julianna pulled the trigger. Ace stood his ground as his chest opened and blood flew out and then he dropped to the floor. Dead.

———

Adrian drove away as the five cop cars passed, heading to the bust. He saw the cars crash through the gate.

The sound of police sirens brought with it a tentative opening of the barn doors. Two cop cars skidded to a halt in front of the girls. The other cars spewed cops to the front and back of the farmhouse. The dogs went racing into the bush.

46

The fella had been shopping. Today was going to be special. Really special. There was a pretty decent suit at the Vinnies that fitted. Paid fifty bucks and conned them into throwing in a shirt and tie. Special. Searched a few second-hand stores before coming across this Vinnies. Lucky he got in when he did. Wouldn't have lasted long hanging there by the counter.

And then there were the flowers. Not any old flowers. Fella was going to take his time with flowers. Special. Had to be special and there were lots of special flowers up the coast. He would make her so happy with the flowers. She'd see he was special.

———

Adrian pulled into the drive. Parked behind the van. Walked up the path to the front door. Knocked. Nothing. Knocked again. Not a movement. Adrian tried looking through the glass front door. Couldn't see bugger-all. Walked along the veranda trying to see in. Looked closer. There was the bugger sitting in a lounge chair staring straight ahead. Didn't he hear? What's his problem?

Adrian yelled out, 'Brian, it's Adrian. Get your arse up and open the door. It's fucking urgent.'

Brian stirred, looked to the window. He could see Adrian. Waved him away.

'Brian, I am not joking. I will call the police. You want that?'

Finally, Brian moved. Stood up and opened the door. Then he turned and went back to his chair.

'What the fuck is wrong with you, mate?'

'She's left me.'

'Who's left you?'

Brian remained silent. Looked like a little boy who'd been grounded.

'Nolene?'

Brian nodded.

'Really?'

And Brian told Adrian the horrid story. He had rung Nolene over and over. She hadn't spoken to him for days. Eventually she answered his call. When he asked her when she'd be back she had replied that she wasn't coming back. Ever. She had moved on. She was sorry but she had found someone new and was starting again. Brian was devastated.

'Karma,' Brian said. 'That'll teach me for fucking around behind her back. What the fuck am I going to do?'

Adrian had no idea but he needed Brian's help. He needed the address of the fella out beyond the pub who he'd sold a property to a few months back.

'I saw him, you know, the other day. Waved to me.'

'Yep, good, Brian, but I need his address.'

Brian picked up his phone. Looked up the fella's address and passed it on to Adrian.

As Adrian dashed out the door, Brian shouted, 'Karma. That's what it was, Adrian. Karma.'

Brian looked down at the strange fucker's address he'd passed on to Adrian, then threw his phone onto the lounge.

47

It was more a fire trail than a road. The odd locked gate every kilometre. Adrian found the fella's place. NO ENTRY loud and clear. Adrian drove past. He hadn't seen the fella's van. Only a house and a shed. A further hundred or so metres on he found a place to park the ute behind two trees. Wouldn't notice it unless you were looking for it. As he finished parking he felt or heard crunching sounds. Got out and looked. The back wheel of the ute sat on a kid's bike. Had to be David's. Or not. Facts not assumptions. Decent assumption though. Adrian felt the adrenaline.

He worked his way back to the fella's entrance. Careful. No. No van. Had to go in. Adrian slid under the barbed wire. Fucking barbed wire. Hated the stuff. Works though. Keeps the cattle in. But not Adrian but maybe David.

Adrian moved across to the shed. Found a peephole and peeped. A GTS Monaro. The one from the classic car show. The one on David's poster. Adrian's supervisor had said a Monaro. Was it the one in the shed? Adrian reached for his phone. Should he ring? Course he should ring. It adds up, doesn't it? Check the house first. Be sure.

So across to the house. Yelled, 'Hey, GT, it's Adrian. Bit broke, mate . . . hoped you might have a job on I could help with.'

Not a sound. Tried again, but nothing. Adrian turned the doorhandle. It was unlocked.

———

The fella had found the perfect garden centre. It had everything. Natives. That's what everybody talked about up here. Gotta have natives. Fella thought they meant the Aboriginals at first. No, it was bloody plants. Native plants. Native to Australia. But some must have come from other places way back. Bloody birds fly across the oceans. Would have dropped seeds. Anyway, great garden centre with great plants and flowers. He mainly wanted white flowers. And he got a bundle. He went a bit mad, he reckoned. Hey, it was for a special occasion. Tulips. White. Camellias. White. Jasmine. White. They even had white roses. He didn't ask if any were native. Didn't give a fuck. They all looked so good. He was a very happy fella as he drove home dressed in his new suit, shirt and tie with his many bunches of white flowers sitting next to him on the passenger seat.

———

Adrian opened the door. This was way above his pay grade. He was undercover. Meant to infiltrate. Find out stuff. This was not on. And he had no warrant.

Had to stop thinking like a cop. He was a bloke looking for work from a mate.

The kitchen was the first room you entered. Messy, but no messier than what you'd find with any bloke living on his own. Adrian moved into the bedroom. Messy again. Clothes on the floor. Unmade bed. Shopping bags lying about, some with dirty clothes in them. Not a filthy room though. Then a laundry bathroom. Nothing special. The usual towel on the floor. Clothes in a corner. Adrian picked up the clothes. There was something not right about them. Shorts and a T-shirt. Far too small to be the fella's. David's?

———

The fella had driven up to the gate. Unlocked it. On the way back to his van he saw the ute buried behind two trees. He knew the ute.

———

Adrian was holding the clothes when the fella smashed him over the head. Adrian dropped to the floor. Out cold.

The fella looked down at Adrian. This was meant to be his special day. He sat beside Adrian, raised his head and howled.

———

Adrian's arms and legs had been bound tight. Being pulled over the rough ground was what brought him to. The fella had dragged him through the house and outside to the yard.

'What's going on, GT? I was looking for you, that's all. I'm not trying to rob you.'

The fella said nothing as he continued to drag Adrian towards the dam.

'GT, honestly, I came looking for more work. Just washed my hands in the bathroom and was drying them on some old clothes of yours.'

'Bullshit.'

'Fair dinkum, mate. Why'd you whack me? I thought we were friends.'

Adrian knew he was in deep shit. If the fella had something to do with David's death then another death wouldn't worry him.

The fella kept dragging Adrian to the dam edge. Adrian struggled but his arms were bound to his body. He could do nothing. And then the fella pushed Adrian's head into the dam. Adrian tried to lift his head. Wrench it from side to side. But no go. The fella was too strong. They say drowning is a lovely way to die. You float off into unconsciousness happy as a pig in shit. That wasn't how Adrian wanted to die. He struggled but he was slipping. Slipping. Slipping.

Suddenly his head was grabbed and hauled out of the dam. He was held up. He began to vomit water. And more water. And cough and cough. How he loved coughing. He would never complain about coughing again. He was alive, with Brian Slaviero standing holding him.

The sarge had a gun in one hand aimed at the fella and was putting cuffs on the fella's wrists with his other hand. None of this made sense. Where the fuck had they come from?

'Where the fuck have you come from? And thank Christ,' Adrian choked out.

But an explanation would have to wait.

'What were you doing here?' the sarge asked as he cut Adrian free.

Adrian tried to explain about the GTS Monaro that was in the shed. How he'd put two and two together. The car and David and the car and the fella. It was David's favourite car.

The sarge had seen the poster.

'Bit thin. Lotta people fancy the Monaro.'

And then Adrian told how he'd found a boy's bike back where he'd parked.

'There are clothes in the bathroom that have to belong to David.'

'Show me.'

Adrian led the way. Brian waited outside while the sarge, Adrian and the fella went into the house. Adrian showed the sarge the shorts and T-shirt.

'Found them down near the beach. Used them as rags to clean the floor. That's all.'

The sarge looked to the fella.

'Sounds like bullshit to me, mate. Enough here for us to have a chat down the station. Let's go.'

Brian was nowhere to be seen as they came from the house and walked towards the gate.

'Brian, we're off. Get your arse into gear.'

They were almost at the gate when Brian caught up.

'Something strange back there, Sarge.'

'Like what?'

It was strange to Brian what he had seen behind the house. He'd sold the house and knew it inside out and upside down, and when he sold it there weren't air vents on the back side of the house.

'Got a secret bunker, have we, mate? Growing weed, are we?'

The fella kept mum.

They all walked back to the house.

'Where's the entrance?'

No need to do a search. They all saw the trapdoor at the same time. Adrian lifted it.

There was the stairway. The sarge had the fella by the belt, forcing him to lead. The sarge followed, then Adrian and Brian.

The sarge saw the keys hanging on the wall and turned to Adrian.

'You open it.'

And Adrian did. He pushed back the wooden door and saw into the room. A room that held a bed and little else except for a young woman dressed in a white wedding dress sitting on the bed facing them.

'I'm Leila,' the young woman in the wedding dress whispered as she stood up and walked towards the men.

She stopped in front of the fella. She looked into his face and smiled.

'This man drowned a boy. I saw him.'

48

Leila was grateful for the sedative. Sleep wasn't going to come easily. She had been taken to the local hospital and checked out. Blood test. Eyes. Throat. Heart rate. The lot. All good, but Leila knew it wasn't the body that would be the problem. It would be upstairs. The mind.

The sarge had contacted her parents. Rung them and gave them a rundown on Leila's nightmare. Told them she was in good hands, then put Leila on the phone. Leila's parents would fly out the next day. Leila was glad. Thought they could all drive together through the red soil of the Australian outback. As she drifted away from the real world, she saw herself in the white wedding dress.

The fella had been taken to Coffs after being charged. He'd be sent to Long Bay jail in Sydney in the coming days. One cop told him he'd be looking at twenty-five years. At least.

Twenty-five years wasn't so bad, he thought. He wouldn't be forgotten, that was for sure. Not by the girl. He knew she'd think about him every single day. Made him smile. And then when he was released he'd dust off the suit and shirt and tie. Always something to look forward to.

Ryan couldn't wait to see Leila. The sarge told him to hold off for a couple of days. Wait until the parents arrived. Let her settle. Ryan agreed. Couldn't believe what she'd been through. He would wait. Meantime he had an email to write. An email to his parents. Mainly his dad. It wasn't easy writing the email talking about sex and sexual identity. Difficult stuff. Hoping that he'd understand and still love him for who he was. Benny was a great help with the email. Ryan decided he would see out the year working for Benny at The Basin and then head back to Paris and then sign up for a stint with Médecins Sans Frontières. Yep, his path was becoming clearer.

———

Anna and the girls were sent back to their homes in South America. It had been a deeply traumatic experience for them all. Julianna and Antonia were examined by a doctor for the abuse they experienced and were told there would be no lasting physical consequences. It's the nightmares they'd have to live with. Anna filled the cops in on the farmhouse where they were held on the way up the coast.

Back home she cut and dyed her hair and moved to São Paulo. She took a job in reception at a large car hire firm and waited. She knew that one day José would come in to hire a car. One day.

———

Ken paid Sergeant Gallagher a visit. Talked through the capture of the fella. About Brian's instinct in ringing the sarge after Adrian had come asking for the fella's address. Talk about good timing. Could've been disastrous for Adrian.

The sarge was glad that David's family now had closure. The family were sure David wouldn't have gone swimming in the ocean at night. They were proved right. Ken hoped the community would come to terms with the terrible events. The murder and the kidnapping. The community needed healing.

Wanda was surprised to learn about Nolene leaving poor Brian, but more surprised when she heard that he had helped in the arrest. Good for Brian. She would leave it a bit before contacting him. He would need some TLC and that she would happily supply. But there was work first. A Newcastle newspaper had been in touch. Someone needed to do a big story on the murder and kidnapping. Why not Wanda? They had liked her article on David. Wanda was pleased.

———

Conchita found running the cafe on her own quite difficult. She needed a partner. She mentioned it to Sheila, who jumped at the chance. She was no dill, Sheila, who had a tidy sum stacked away. Twenty thousand dollars to buy in. And in she was. Adrian would need to find himself another cleaner. Sheila would make sure it was a bloke.

———

The supervisor and Adrian had fish and chips and a beer on the deck of the Icebergs at Bondi. Beautiful day. Blue sky, blue ocean.

The supervisor filled Adrian in on the sex-trafficking bust. A very successful bust. The girls had helped by taking out Ace and making a bloody mess of the Don. The other men had surrendered peacefully. The girls were in good nick and sent home. The Don was very useful once his health improved.

Funny thing was he would only have male nurses see to him. Any sign of a woman and he would freak out. The supervisor thought that might take a while to change with the Don. However, he was happy to spill the beans on the crime syndicate running the show. Several arrests were in progress.

'Did you get the third bikie? The bloke who drove out in the ute before you all arrived?'

'What bikie? There was no third bikie.'

'I gave you the rego.'

'Don't know what you're talking about.' The supervisor took a sip of his beer. 'No rego, no third bikie.'

Adrian nodded. He smiled. 'No third bikie. Right.'

The supervisor suggested that Adrian might find another supplier of weed for Benny.

'Never know where it will lead to.'

Adrian said he'd think about it. Wasn't sure Benny would be up for it again.

The supervisor and Adrian finished their fish and chips, downed their beers, shook hands and left the Icebergs.

———

The earth hadn't yet settled. Moira placed her flowers on the mound. Her David's mound, covering the box that held his remains. His sweet remains. She had been every day since the funeral. Marcia and Wayne knelt by the mound.

Moira spoke quietly.

'They caught him, David. It doesn't bring you back but it was important he was caught.'

Then Wayne put his palm on the mound.

'Learnin' our language, little brother. Learnin' it for you. Love ya, mate.'

Marcia placed an arm around her grandmother.

———

The waves were about head high and a little full. Rolling in from the Point down to the clubhouse some four hundred metres away. Great mal waves. Ken took off on a beauty, made a turn just as Adrian dropped in and turned. Then Brian dropped in.

Benny was paddling out when he saw the three of them on the same wave. He turned, paddled hard for it and dropped in on Brian.

Brian smiled. Karma. They rode the wave together.

Acknowledgements

The Drowning owes its life to some great and generous people. Same with *Sweet Jimmy*, I sought the experience of Detective Chief Superintendent Darren Bennett of the NSW Police Force, and this time his colleague Commander Hilda Sirec of the AFP. Your help in keeping me on 'the straight and narrow' was invaluable.

Gary Williams and Micklo Jarrett at the Muurrbay Aboriginal Language and Culture Co-operative at Nambucca Heads in New South Wales made dealing with a difficult subject that much easier. As did Kevin Williams at the Aboriginal Legal Service in Kempsey, NSW.

Alexandra Brown and Alison Jones at the Sydney office of Médecins Sans Frontières opened my eyes to their extraordinary work worldwide.

Rod Soares, my son Joe's surfer mate from Brazil, helped me layer South America into the story.

And thanks to my mate Gavin Oakey, who can fix or build anything.

Richard Walsh, Annette Barlow, Angela Handley and Peri Wilson at Allen & Unwin kept me afloat.

To all of you, thank you.

Now I just have to get my family to read *The Drowning*.

Also by Bryan Brown

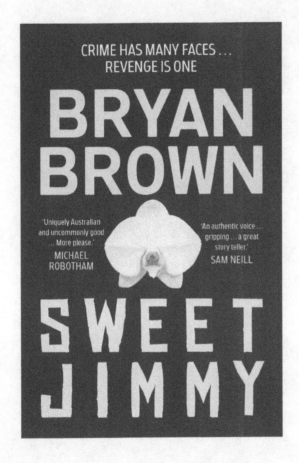

CRIME HAS MANY FACES . . .
REVENGE IS ONE

BRYAN BROWN

'Uniquely Australian
and uncommonly good
. . . More please.'
MICHAEL
ROBOTHAM

'An authentic voice . . .
gripping . . . a great
story teller.'
SAM NEILL

SWEET JIMMY